Acting Edition

Prayer for the French Republic

by Joshua Harmon

Copyright © 2024 by Joshua Harmon
All Rights Reserved

PRAYER FOR THE FRENCH REPUBLIC is fully protected under the copyright laws of the United States of America, the British Commonwealth, including Canada, and all member countries of the Berne Convention for the Protection of Literary and Artistic Works, the Universal Copyright Convention, and/or the World Trade Organization conforming to the Agreement on Trade Related Aspects of Intellectual Property Rights. All rights, including professional and amateur stage productions, recitation, lecturing, public reading, motion picture, radio broadcasting, television, online/digital production, and the rights of translation into foreign languages are strictly reserved.

ISBN 978-0-573-71114-5

www.concordtheatricals.com
www.concordtheatricals.co.uk

FOR PRODUCTION INQUIRIES

UNITED STATES AND CANADA
info@concordtheatricals.com
1-866-979-0447

UNITED KINGDOM AND EUROPE
licensing@concordtheatricals.co.uk
020-7054-7298

Each title is subject to availability from Concord Theatricals Corp., depending upon country of performance. Please be aware that *PRAYER FOR THE FRENCH REPUBLIC* may not be licensed by Concord Theatricals Corp. in your territory. Professional and amateur producers should contact the nearest Concord Theatricals Corp. office or licensing partner to verify availability.

CAUTION: Professional and amateur producers are hereby warned that *PRAYER FOR THE FRENCH REPUBLIC* is subject to a licensing fee. The purchase, renting, lending or use of this book does not constitute a license to perform this title(s), which license must be obtained from Concord Theatricals Corp. prior to any performance. Performance of this title(s) without a license is a violation of federal law and may subject the producer and/or presenter of such performances to civil penalties. Both amateurs and professionals considering a production are strongly advised to apply to the appropriate agent before starting rehearsals, advertising, or booking a theatre. A licensing fee must be paid whether the title(s) is presented for charity or gain and whether or not admission is charged. Professional/Stock licensing fees are quoted upon application to Concord Theatricals Corp.

This work is published by Samuel French, an imprint of Concord Theatricals Corp.

No one shall make any changes in this title(s) for the purpose of production. No part of this book may be reproduced, stored in a retrieval system, scanned, uploaded, or transmitted in any form, by any means, now known or yet to be invented, including mechanical, electronic, digital, photocopying, recording, videotaping, or otherwise, without the prior written permission of the publisher. No one shall share this title(s), or any part of this title(s), through any social media or file hosting websites.

For all inquiries regarding motion picture, television, online/digital and other media rights, please contact Concord Theatricals Corp.

MUSIC AND THIRD-PARTY MATERIALS USE NOTE

Licensees are solely responsible for obtaining formal written permission from copyright owners to use copyrighted music and/or other copyrighted third-party materials (e.g. artworks, logos) in the performance of this play and are strongly cautioned to do so. If no such permission is obtained by the licensee, then the licensee must use only original music and materials that the licensee owns and controls. Licensees are solely responsible and liable for clearances of all third-party copyrighted materials, including without limitation music, and shall indemnify the copyright owners of the play(s) and their licensing agent, Concord Theatricals Corp., against any costs, expenses, losses and liabilities arising from the use of such copyrighted third-party materials by licensees. For music, please contact the appropriate music licensing authority in your territory for the rights to any incidental music.

IMPORTANT BILLING AND CREDIT REQUIREMENTS

If you have obtained performance rights to this title, please refer to your licensing agreement for important billing and credit requirements.

"I THOUGHT ABOUT YOU"
Written by James Van Heusen and Johnny Mercer
Published in the United States and Canada by Range Road Music Inc.
(ASCAP) and WC Music Corp. (ASCAP).
Published in the British Reversionary Territories by Bourne Co.
and WC Music Corp. (ASCAP).
Published in the rest of the world by Bourne Co.
All rights reserved. Used with permission from Round Hill Music,
Bourne Co. and Warner Chappell Music.

"FOREVER YOUNG"
Words and Music by Bob Dylan
© Universal Tunes (SESAC)
All rights reserved.

PRAYER FOR THE FRENCH REPUBLIC was originally commissioned by the Manhattan Theatre Club (Lynne Meadow, Artistic Director; Barry Grove, Executive Producer) with funds provided by Bank of America and received its world premiere at New York City Center Stage I on February 1, 2022. The performance was directed by David Cromer, with scenic design by Takeshi Kata, costume design by Sarah Laux, lighting design by Amith Chandrashaker, sound design by Lee Kinney, original music and sound design by Daniel Kluger, and hair and makeup design by J. Jared Janas. The production stage manager was Richard A. Hodge, and the stage manager was Ashley-Rose Galligan. The cast was as follows:

MARCELLE SALOMON BENHAMOU . . . . Betsy Aidem

CHARLES BENHAMOU . . . . Jeff Seymour

ELODIE BENHAMOU . . . . Francis Benhamou

DANIEL BENHAMOU . . . . Yair Ben-Dor

PATRICK SALOMON . . . . Richard Topol

MOLLY . . . . Molly Ranson

PIERRE SALOMON . . . . Pierre Epstein

IRMA SALOMON . . . . Nancy Robinette

ADOLPHE SALOMON . . . . Kenneth Tigar

LUCIEN SALOMON . . . . Ari Brand

YOUNG PIERRE SALOMON . . . . Peyton Lusk

PRAYER FOR THE FRENCH REPUBLIC was produced on Broadway by the Manhattan Theatre Club (Lynne Meadow, Artistic Director; Chris Jennings, Executive Producer) and opened at the Samuel J. Friedman Theatre on January 9, 2024. The cast was as follows:

MARCELLE SALOMON BENHAMOU . . . . Betsy Aidem
CHARLES BENHAMOU . . . . Nael Nacer
ELODIE BENHAMOU . . . . Francis Benhamou
DANIEL BENHAMOU . . . . Aria Shahghasemi
PATRICK SALOMON . . . . Anthony Edwards
MOLLY . . . . Molly Ranson
PIERRE SALOMON . . . . Richard Masur
IRMA SALOMON . . . . Nancy Robinette
ADOLPHE SALOMON . . . . Daniel Oreskes
LUCIEN SALOMON . . . . Ari Brand
YOUNG PIERRE SALOMON . . . . Ethan Haberfield

PRAYER FOR THE FRENCH REPUBLIC is the inaugural winner of the Theater J Trish Vradenburg Jewish Play Prize (Adam Immerwahr, Artistic Director; Jojo Ruf, Managing Director).

PRAYER FOR THE FRENCH REPUBLIC was developed as part of the Martha Heasley Cox Virgin Play Festival at Magic Theatre in San Francisco (Loretta Greco, Artistic Director).

CHARACTERS

2016–2017

MARCELLE SALOMON BENHAMOU – 50s

CHARLES BENHAMOU – 50s, Marcelle's husband

ELODIE BENHAMOU – 28, their daughter

DANIEL BENHAMOU – 26, their son

PATRICK SALOMON – 50s, Marcelle's brother

MOLLY – 20, a distant American cousin

PIERRE SALOMON – 80s, Marcelle and Patrick's father

1944–1946

IRMA SALOMON – 70s, Pierre's grandmother

ADOLPHE SALOMON – 70s, Pierre's grandfather

LUCIEN SALOMON – 40s, Pierre's father

YOUNG PIERRE SALOMON – at age 15

SETTING

Paris, France.

TIME

2016–2017 and 1944–1946

For my parents

"If 100,000 Frenchmen of Spanish origin were to leave, I would never say that France is no longer France. But if 100,000 Jews leave, France will no longer be France. The French Republic will be judged a failure."

– Manuel Valls, Prime Minister of France, in January 2015,
just after the attacks on Charlie Hebdo
and the kosher supermarket

ACT ONE

(A lone piano onstage.)

*(***PATRICK*** *enters, takes in the piano for a bit, then turns to us.)*

PATRICK. My father owns a piano store, on Rue du Faubourg Montmartre. He's the fifth – and last – generation to run the place. Pianos Salomon – that's our family name, Salomon – was founded by my great-great-great-grandfather in 1855. Owning a piano used to be something you strived for, a sign you'd made it to the middle class, but it doesn't hold the same appeal anymore. Most days my father sits in an empty store, an old man waiting for customers who almost never show. He's in his late eighties, but he won't give the place up.

Sometimes, a friend will ask how come my sister and I don't take over the business. Five generations! All that history! Think of what the store has seen – and survived! But it's not how either of us want to spend our time, and besides, you can't support a family selling pianos, not really.

This is a Salomon original. Our name's on the fallboard. They used to manufacture them, Papa only sells them now. This one belongs to Marcelle...

I'd say let's start at the beginning, but what's the beginning of a family? We've been in France more than a thousand years. So let's start here: it's early fall. It's late afternoon, sixteen years into the twenty-first century. My sister's welcoming a distant American cousin of ours into her home, in the heart of Paris.

1

(**MARCELLE** *enters with* **MOLLY,** *as* **PATRICK** *disappears into the darkness.*)

MARCELLE. So my great-grandmother, Irma, was sisters with your great-great-grandmother, Lucie. They were born in the east, in Strasbourg, then moved west, to remain French, when Alsace–Lorraine became German for about fifty years. Then Lucie left France, and went to America, but she stayed in touch, very close, with her sister Irma, and then Lucie had a daughter in New York, whose name escapes me but who is your great-grandmother, and Irma had a son in Lille, named Lucien, who was my grandfather, and they were cousins, and then your grandmother Renee was born, and my grandfather had Pierre, who is my father, and so I am cousins with your mother, and you are cousins with my children.

MOLLY. Right.

(Quick beat.)

Say that again?

MARCELLE. We'll go backwards. You are cousins with my children. I am cousins with your mother.

MOLLY. Right.

MARCELLE. My father is Pierre, your grandmother is Renee, and they are cousins.

MOLLY. OK.

MARCELLE. And their grandmothers were Irma and Lucie, and they were sisters. That's the connection.

MOLLY. In Strasbourg.

MARCELLE. First Strasbourg, then Lille, then Paris. You follow me?

MOLLY. Yes. No. Sort of.

MARCELLE. The details are not important.

MOLLY. Basically, we're cousins.

MARCELLE. We're cousins.

MOLLY. But not first cousins?

MARCELLE. No. No. Uh… I don't know how it works, exactly? Third cousins? Fourth? It's distant, but…

MOLLY. Yeah I don't really get the whole cousin thing.

MARCELLE. We share blood. We both descend from the man who founded Pianos Salomon. See? That's our name there.

> (**MARCELLE** *points out their name on the fallboard.*)

This was my great-grandmother's.

MOLLY. I thought your name was uhm, Ben, Ben uhm…

MARCELLE. Benhamou, yes, that's my married name, my maiden name is Salomon.

MOLLY. Uh huh.

MARCELLE. I can try to explain it in English, if you prefer –

MOLLY. No, please. Just French. I'm trying, I want to get as fluent as I can.

MARCELLE. You speak very well, I have to say.

MOLLY. Thank you. I feel like, I have such a long way to go, but –

MARCELLE. No, your French is very good.

MOLLY. Thank you. In school, they made us choose: French or Spanish, but my mom was like, "There's no choice in this family: you're taking French." Everyone still fancies themselves, uhm, very French, even though no one on my side of the family has been, uh, French for, uh, a hundred years.

MARCELLE. And you're here for a year?

MOLLY. A school year, yeah.

MARCELLE. In Nantes?

MOLLY. Yeah. It's like, two hours from here, by train?

MARCELLE. I know where Nantes is.

MOLLY. Right. Of course. Sorry.

MARCELLE. You didn't want to study in Paris?

MOLLY. I did but my school – they don't really encourage it.

MARCELLE. Why not?

MOLLY. I think they're trying to break the whole entitled Americans in Paris thing. My parents didn't want me to come to France at all, but...

MARCELLE. Why not?

MOLLY. Just cause of all the, you know. The terrorism.

MARCELLE. There's terrorism everywhere.

MOLLY. That's what I said, but they were scared.

MARCELLE. Aren't you from New York? What's to be scared?

MOLLY. I agree.

MARCELLE. The whole world has terrorism now. There's nowhere to hide. Either you live in the world, or you live in a cave. Personally, I don't want to be a caveman.

MOLLY. Exactly. But, they felt better if I was in a smaller city. And it's nice, totally ni... My host family is kind of... uhm, what's the word I want? They're not racist, but...

MARCELLE. Uh huh.

MOLLY. They're not *not* racist. But, at the same time, I have to live with them for a year, so I need to just...

So my Mom said, why don't you visit our family in Paris, which, I didn't really know we had, I knew my nana wrote letters to France, I guess to your mother, right?

MARCELLE. No. To Philippe and Francine.

MOLLY. Oh.

MARCELLE. My father's cousins. They got out before the war.

MOLLY. Oh OK.

MARCELLE. But Francine is dead. And Philippe's in Switzerland now, most of the time, so he asked if I would –

MOLLY. But you stayed in France, during the war?

MARCELLE. I was not born before World War II.

MOLLY. Oh.

MARCELLE. I'm not *that* old.

MOLLY. Oh, I'm sorry, I didn't –

MARCELLE. But yes, my family stayed.

MOLLY. Wow. It's so… it's unbelievable, to have French family.

MARCELLE. OK.

> (*In the hallway behind them,* **ELODIE** *walks past, from her bedroom to the bathroom. She looks like she's been asleep for a thousand years, disheveled and exhausted.* **MARCELLE** *waits for* **ELODIE** *to introduce herself, but she says nothing and exits, as* **MOLLY** *watches.*)

So you will make yourself at home. Come and go as you please this weekend.

MOLLY. Thank you.

MARCELLE. I'm not usually home this early, but I'm moving offices, and they're painting today, so…

MOLLY. What do you do?

MARCELLE. I'm a doctor, now a professor, and after three completely inept department heads, they finally realized, "Oh. Maybe a woman can run this department." Hence, the new office.

MOLLY. Congratulations.

MARCELLE. Thank you. So you will have dinner with us tonight?

MOLLY. Sure, yes, thank you.

MARCELLE. We are not strict here, but traditional, so...

MOLLY. I don't... I don't follow.

MARCELLE. We're traditional. You know. We light the candles, Shabbat dinner, you know.

MOLLY. I still don't...

MARCELLE. Shabbat. You don't understand me. Shabbat?

MOLLY. Do you mean, like, *Shabbat*?

MARCELLE. Yes. Shabbat.

MOLLY. Ohhhh. OK.

MARCELLE. Do you keep Shabbat?

MOLLY. Uhm, no, no I don't. But I'm not really, you know...

MARCELLE. Not what?

MOLLY. I wasn't, I mean, I wasn't raised with any religion...

MARCELLE. But you're Jewish, no?

MOLLY. I guess technically? But I don't believe in organized religion, I actually think if we could, uhm, end all religions immediately we *might* have a chance at saving our planet but I, I *totally* respect if you want to. Believe. It's just, not for me.

> *(Beat.)*

MARCELLE. Well. Welcome.

   (**ELODIE** *walks past the room, slowly.*)

Elodie? You want to say hello to our American cousin? This is Molly.

ELODIE. Hello.

   (**ELODIE** *exits.*)

MOLLY. Nice to meet you!

   (*Beat.*)

MARCELLE. Elodie is quite… tired.

MOLLY. Yeah.

MARCELLE. She's not – very tired.

MOLLY. It's such a pretty name, Elodie.

MARCELLE. Yes, it is. Excuse me, I need to check on dinner.

MOLLY. OK. So, is there, uhm – am I OK, to come to, whatever, like this?

MARCELLE. Yes, you're dressed fine. It's just dinner, here. Just us. We're just traditional.

MOLLY. Right.

What does that mean?

MARCELLE. We keep the traditions. My son is a little more religious, but we – I myself, my brother and I were raised almost with nothing. But, this is to be expected, after the war, many Jews just…

   (**MARCELLE** *makes a quick gesture with her hands, indicating that they gave it up.*)

Then I met my husband. I wasn't looking for a Jewish husband, this was irrelevant for me at the time, but we met, we fell in love, despite our differences, and –

MOLLY. Differences?

MARCELLE. Well he is Sephardic, he comes from – his family is from Algeria.

MOLLY. Really!

MARCELLE. Yes, really.

MOLLY. That's interesting.

MARCELLE. Most Jews in France today, the vast majority, their roots are North African. It's very common.

MOLLY. I didn't know that.

MARCELLE. Yes.

MOLLY. Why is that?

MARCELLE. They came in the 60s.

MOLLY. Why?

MARCELLE. Because. It stopped being safe.

Many, many centuries they lived there, and then…

(Quick beat.)

Anyway. The sofa is very comfortable, no one complains.

MOLLY. It's great. I'm already, so comfortable.

MARCELLE. I'm sorry I don't have a spare bedroom to offer but –

MOLLY. This is fine!

MARCELLE. I did not think, at this point in my life I would still have a full house, but –

MOLLY. This is fine. This is – Thank you.

> *(**MARCELLE** exits into the kitchen. **MOLLY** is alone. She takes in the room, then approaches the piano, maybe touches it.)*

(After a moment, the front door opens offstage.)

CHARLES. *(Offstage.)* Marcelle?

MARCELLE. *(Offstage.)* I'm in the kitchen.

*(**CHARLES** enters, sees **MOLLY**, but ignores her and exits into the kitchen. We hear him and **MARCELLE** speaking offstage.)*

*(Then **DANIEL** appears. He wears a kippah. He is bloodied. Dried blood on his shirt collar, dried blood coming out of his nose. He looks at **MOLLY**. She looks at him. They say nothing.)*

*(**MARCELLE** and **CHARLES** burst out of the kitchen.)*

Oh my god! Daniel what happened –

DANIEL. I'm fine, I'm –

MARCELLE. What happened? Look at you.

CHARLES. He got beat up.

MARCELLE. You were what?

CHARLES. I just saw him outside, stumbling into the apartment.

MARCELLE. This happened outside?

DANIEL. No, in Sarcelles. I'm OK.

MARCELLE. Are you OK?

DANIEL. I'm OK.

MARCELLE. What did the police do?

DANIEL. I didn't, I didn't see the police.

MARCELLE. You didn't go to the police?

DANIEL. No –

MARCELLE. Call the police.

DANIEL. No! Don't call the police.

MARCELLE. I'm calling the police!

DANIEL. DO NOT call the police. No. I don't want to –

MARCELLE. Why can't we call the police?

DANIEL. Because Mom, not now. I just need to –

(**ELODIE** *emerges.*)

MARCELLE. Who did this to you?

CHARLES. Who do you think!

ELODIE. What's happening?

MARCELLE. Your brother got beat up.

ELODIE. What?

DANIEL. They just roughed me up a little.

MARCELLE. This is what we call roughed up? Did they break your nose?

DANIEL. Ow.

MARCELLE. Let's go to the hospital.

CHARLES. Let me look at him.

MARCELLE. But don't you think we should take him to the hospital?

DANIEL. I don't need to go to the hospital, nothing's broken I –

CHARLES. Sit down, let me see, let me take a look.

MARCELLE. Wait, not on the sofa you're all bloody.

CHARLES. Not on the sofa! Who cares about the sofa!

MARCELLE. Because not on the sofa!

CHARLES. Oh for God's sake, fine, let's go to the bathroom.

> (**CHARLES, MARCELLE, DANIEL,** *and* **ELODIE** *walk down the hall to the bathroom, which is just offstage. We hear everything.* **MOLLY** *stays in the living room, watching, unsure of what to do.)*

MARCELLE. *(Offstage.)* How do you know you don't need to go to the hospital?

DANIEL. *(Offstage.)* Because I didn't break anything.

MARCELLE. *(Offstage.)* How do you know?

DANIEL. *(Offstage.)* I can tell.

CHARLES. *(Offstage.)* Marcelle, can I take a look at him?

MARCELLE. *(Offstage.)* You're not an orthopedic surgeon.

CHARLES. *(Offstage.)* I'm a doctor.

MARCELLE. *(Offstage.)* So am I!

CHARLES. *(Offstage.)* You're a psychiatrist, can I take a look at him?

MARCELLE. *(Offstage.)* So take a look at him! Who's stopping you?

CHARLES. *(Offstage.)* Sit down, son. Can you sit?

DANIEL. *(Offstage.)* Yeah I can sit.

ELODIE. *(Offstage.)* What happened?

DANIEL. *(Offstage.)*

I was leaving school, I was walking to the metro, these three guys came up and started saying, "Hey Jew, fuckin Jew," things like that.	**CHARLES**. *(Offstage.)* Sit still.

DANIEL. *(Offstage.)* I didn't say anything but they kept following me and then before I knew what was happening they started – Because I don't want to wear a baseball cap I –

CHARLES. *(Offstage.)* Sit still stop moving.

DANIEL. *(Offstage.)* I'm not going to change my behavior because there are bigots in the world, I'm not –

MARCELLE. *(Offstage.)* How many times have I begged you to wear a baseball cap? Why do you do this, why do you insist on putting yourself in harm's way for no reason! There's no reason!

Listen to yourself! Are you even listening to yourself, what you're saying!

ELODIE. *(Offstage.)* Can you let him finish? What happened?

DANIEL. *(Offstage.)* They followed me, they grabbed me, they punched me, a few times.

MARCELLE. *(Offstage.)* A few times!

DANIEL. *(Offstage.)* A few times. That was it.

MARCELLE. *(Offstage.)* That was it!

DANIEL. *(Offstage.)* It really wasn't a big deal –

MARCELLE. *(Offstage.)* Not a big deal! No, it's perfectly normal to get punched in the face on a Friday afternoon, walking to the metro, that's perfectly normal –

CHARLES. *(Offstage.)* Does that hurt?

DANIEL. *(Offstage.)* No, I told you, I'm fine –

CHARLES. *(Offstage.)* How about that? How's that feel?

DANIEL. *(Offstage.)* It's sore when you press on it, but –

MARCELLE. *(Offstage.)* Sore! Oh my god!

CHARLES. *(Offstage.)* Marcelle you need to relax or I'm going to...

MARCELLE. *(Offstage.)* Going to what?

CHARLES. *(Offstage.)* Just, calm down.

MARCELLE. *(Offstage.)* OK fine! I'll calm down! I'll calm down! Great! Fine! Fine! Great! I'm calming down! Let's all calm down while my son bleeds to death in the bathroom.

CHARLES. *(Offstage.)* Marcelle.

Make a little space. Take a step back. OK?

> **(MARCELLE** *and* **ELODIE** *become visible now in the hallway, as they inch away from the bathroom.)*

(Offstage.) Nothing seems broken to me.

DANIEL. *(Offstage.)* I know.

> *(A beat.)*

MARCELLE. I'm gonna call the police.

DANIEL. *(Offstage.)* Mom! Stop!

ELODIE. Why should she stop?

MARCELLE. Why should I stop? Reporting a crime, is a crime now?

DANIEL. *(Offstage.)* I didn't even get a good look at them, it happened so fast.

MARCELLE. This never happened until you started dressing like this. You never had a problem before.

CHARLES. *(Offstage.)* Stop yelling at the boy –

MARCELLE. You put a huge target on your back! Here I am! Here I am! Now is not the moment to walk around with a sign that says "Here I Am" on your back it's not the time!

DANIEL. *(Offstage.)* The sun is setting.

MARCELLE. Now is not the – what?

DANIEL. *(Offstage.)* The sun is setting.

(Beat. They all return to the living room.)

MARCELLE. You're covered in blood.

DANIEL. I'm not covered –

MARCELLE. You're covered –

CHARLES. He's OK. He didn't break anything. It's just a little –

DANIEL. Everyone! Enough! Please. Can we please light the candles before the sun goes down? Please?

*(A beat. Then **MARCELLE** gets two candles, in silver candlesticks, and puts them on the piano. She takes some matches. The others stand to the side.)*

CHARLES. Are you Marcelle's cousin?

MOLLY. Hi, yes, I'm Molly?

CHARLES. Welcome.

MOLLY. Thanks.

*(**MARCELLE** puts a napkin over her head, then lights the two candles. The **FAMILY** gathers closer, but no one is touching. There is space between them. It's uncomfortable. **MOLLY** stands to the side.)*

MARCELLE. Baruch atah Adonai, Eloheinu melech ha'olam, asher kid'shanu b'mitzvotav, v'tzivanu l'hadlik ner shel Shabbat.

*(**MARCELLE** moves her hands over the candles, her eyes still closed. Then she looks up at her son, takes him in for a moment.)*

CHARLES. Gut shabbes.

MARCELLE. *(Breathless.)* Yeah.

> *(No one knows what to do.* **MARCELLE** *stares at her son, then grabs him and pulls him close. He holds onto her.)*

You must have been so scared.

> *(He half-nods. She takes his face in her hands.)*

Let me call the police, OK?

DANIEL. Mom. No.

MARCELLE. But sweetie, why?

DANIEL. Because.

MARCELLE. Because why?

DANIEL. Because I don't want – I've seen what happens – Everyone… you're not just a person anymore, you become this thing, who's been through something. Even if it's not…

My students are already on edge. I don't want to be the reason they feel even more insecure. And besides.

I really didn't get a good look. I wouldn't even be able to describe them. So they'd write it up, it'd be in the news, and then it's all anyone would talk about but that's not what I… and then even then, after all that, it wouldn't change a thing, so there's no point.

MARCELLE. But you don't think, it's important, for them to keep track of things like this?

DANIEL. I'm not doing it. So.

CHARLES. Do you want to – does he have time to get cleaned up, before dinner?

MARCELLE. He has time of course he has –

CHARLES. Do you want to take a shower, wash off? I think you'll feel better.

DANIEL. Yeah. OK.

MARCELLE. That's a good idea.

DANIEL. But honestly? And I mean this… I'm done talking about this tonight. OK?

> (**DANIEL** *waits a second for someone to agree. But no one does. He exits. Once he is offstage:)*

MARCELLE. We have to talk to him, we have to talk to him tonight, this stops now, this stops tonight –

CHARLES. Maybe this isn't the moment to have this conversation –

MARCELLE. He wants to dress like a maniac? In the house, be my guest. But when he goes outside, it stops.

CHARLES. And how do you propose we enforce that? He's twenty-six years old –

MARCELLE. We just do! Then he can't live here if he's going to… Where is his – Why can't he be private? Religion is not something to advertise, that's not how we – He wasn't raised that way, he –

ELODIE. Don't you think it's a problem, that a person can't go outside wearing something on his head for fear of being attacked?

MARCELLE. Of course it's a problem but you don't solve a problem by exacerbating a problem that's not how you solve a problem.

ELODIE. So how do you propose solving this problem?

MARCELLE. And you certainly don't do it in neighborhoods where you know there's a high risk of being attacked. Then you're just asking for it.

ELODIE. Oh so Daniel's asking for it now? Is that seriously your argument? He's asking for it?

MARCELLE. Elodie, I am *so* not in the mood for your *shit* tonight.

CHARLES. Let's all just stop it please! Just stop it! I can't even think. Please.

> *(Beat.)*

Let's get dinner on the table, OK? Let's have dinner.

> *(Beat.)*

Let's have – Let's have dinner.

> *(But no one moves.)*

MOLLY. I – I don't know if I mentioned, I'm a vegetarian?

> *(The lights fade on the **BENHAMOUS** and come up on **PATRICK**, at the lip of the stage.)*

PATRICK. More than seventy years earlier, in 1944, on the other side of Paris, in a modest apartment on the Boulevard Beaumarchais, an elderly couple sit down to a meal.

> *(**IRMA** and **ADOLPHE** enter, and sit at a dining room table. **ADOLPHE** is nearly blind.)*

These are my great-grandparents. Their names are Irma and Adolphe. It's their piano Marcelle inherited. Which is fine. I'm not bitter.

The story goes, the SS sent someone to arrest them, but their building's super grabbed him and said, "What are you doing, it's old people, leave them alone." And he did. He left, and Irma and Adolphe spent the war in their apartment in Paris, untouched.

They have three grown children. Jacqueline got out with her family before the war and fled to Cuba. But Robert was arrested in '42, Lucien in '43, along with his wife and three children.

There's no mail service, no telegrams, no phone calls. For the last year, Irma and Adolphe haven't heard a word about their children. They know nothing.

And I know almost nothing about them. I didn't ask questions as a kid. I know just a handful of details: They were first cousins – people married their cousins in those days. I know Adolphe was nearly blind, and Irma had won first prize at a piano conservatory when she was young. I know they'd tried to make it in America, but couldn't scrounge up any work, so they came back to France and took over the family business.

But these are just facts. What were they like, as people? Papa had just one anecdote: When he was little, Irma would butter his bread, then scrape her knife against his piece of bread to get butter for hers. She'd survived World War I, the Great Depression. She'd learned to economize.

> (**IRMA** *has been buttering bread for* **ADOLPHE**.
> *She scrapes her knife against his slice, takes
> butter for her own, then puts* **ADOLPHE**'s *slice
> on his plate.*)

And this stayed with me for a long time. To think – all anyone remembers when you're gone is this tiny gesture, this trick you taught yourself, when you were one small person facing the giant forces of history.

What did they talk about? I have to imagine it was hard not to talk about their children, their grandchildren...

IRMA. We don't talk about our children that much.

ADOLPHE. Oh?

IRMA. We don't.

ADOLPHE. Irma.

IRMA. What?

ADOLPHE. That's not entirely the truth.

IRMA. Well, of course, I talk about them sometimes. They're my children.

PATRICK. Where do you think they are?

IRMA. Somewhere safe, I hope.

ADOLPHE. We don't know, we really don't.

IRMA. Jacqueline and her family went to Cuba, before they stopped letting people out. Of course, Max begged Lucien to go with them –

ADOLPHE. Irma, don't –

IRMA. I'm just explaining, because Lucien had the piano business, his money was all in those pianos, he couldn't just leave but if he had gone to Cuba when they begged him –

ADOLPHE. I can't rehash this again, I can't –

> (*Somehow in these lines,* **PATRICK** *disappears, and we are just with* **IRMA** *and* **ADOLPHE,** *in the past.*)

IRMA. Because they begged him, Jacqueline begged him –

ADOLPHE. Irma –

IRMA. Max said he could get them visas, Max said he could –

ADOLPHE. Irma please.

IRMA. If they had gone to Cuba, they'd be celebrating Pierre's – you know it's his fourteenth birthday today – they'd be celebrating at… maybe at the beach! Maybe at the beach!

ADOLPHE. Please stop, darling. Please.

IRMA. Maybe in the ocean! Doesn't that sound marvelous? To turn fourteen in the ocean, in Cuba? Then they could all get together, the whole family, all the cousins and have birthday cake with Pierre. In Havana.

ADOLPHE. Even when they all lived in Paris they didn't celebrate birthdays together.

IRMA. Sometimes they did.

ADOLPHE. They never did. They fought too much. And I assure you: if they were in Havana, they would be fighting still.

IRMA. You don't know that.

ADOLPHE. I know.

IRMA. It was an idea.

ADOLPHE. It's a fantasy.

IRMA. So what?

ADOLPHE. Alright.

IRMA. They won't forget to celebrate his birthday, will they?

ADOLPHE. I know as much as you.

IRMA. But what are they doing for his birthday?

ADOLPHE. I don't know!

IRMA. But how are they celebrating?

ADOLPHE. I don't know how they're celebrating!

IRMA. Fine! Forget it.

ADOLPHE. I don't know where they are!

IRMA. I said, forget it.

ADOLPHE. For all I know –

IRMA. Forget! It!

(Beat.)

ADOLPHE. They are in a small apartment, somewhere in the mountains.

*(**IRMA** stops to listen.)*

After they were arrested, they spent a few nights in Paris, then they got away and went to the mountains. Somewhere safe. That's where they are.

IRMA. In the mountains.

ADOLPHE. Yes. It's very beautiful where they are. And Lucien's found work tuning pianos.

IRMA. He has?

ADOLPHE. Yes. He tunes pianos. There's a music school nearby, so he has a lot of work. And the school even has a few Salomon pianos, so he goes to work, he tunes the pianos, he sees our name and thinks of us, and all our stores all over France.

IRMA. Twenty-two stores, Adolphe.

ADOLPHE. Twenty-two stores. And as he tunes them, he thinks about how one day, he will teach his son to run the stores, then Pierre will take over and the stores will go on forever.

IRMA. They will.

ADOLPHE. And Eva has taken in some sewing, so between the two of them, they're getting by. It's cold in the mountains, but they're fine. And the children are in school, they're doing well, even Colette.

IRMA. OK, that I don't believe. Colette's sweet but... *(Unspoken: not that bright.)*

ADOLPHE. Well, she's taking her studies seriously, for once. And this morning Pierre woke in their apartment in the mountains and turned fourteen. Eva saved her rations to bake him a cake, it isn't very sweet, there isn't much sugar, but he has a cake, and Lucien bought him a Swiss Army knife so that when he's in the woods hiking with his friends if he needs to cut through a rope or whatever boys do at that age, he will have a little knife in his pocket he can take out.

IRMA. And Robert is… Robert is alright too.

ADOLPHE. He's alright. He's… working for France. Making buttons.

IRMA. Buttons?

ADOLPHE. When the war is over, France will give him a medal.

IRMA. They already gave him a medal, for the Great War.

ADOLPHE. Well now he will have two. And our children will come home, we'll all be together, and everyone will get along beautifully.

(Quick beat. They both laugh.)

IRMA. That's funny.

ADOLPHE. It's your fantasy…

IRMA. No, they'll come home, after about ten minutes they'll start arguing, and I'll yell, "Robert! Please! You haven't seen your brother in four years!"

ADOLPHE. Then Jacqueline will encourage Colette not to take a second piece of cake, Colette will start to cry, Eva will ask what happened and she'll say Aunt Jacqueline called me fat, and Eva will say don't you call my daughter fat don't you dare and Jacqueline will say I never said she was fat I just know she's been unhappy with her weight I was trying to encourage her, then Eva will storm off and you'll have to console Jacqueline because she'll be quite upset and she'll say I try and I try but no matter what I do it's never right it's never enough I give up. And that's how the reunion will go.

(Beat.)

IRMA. I can't wait.

(Later that night.)

(In the transition, **MARCELLE** *and* **CHARLES** *throw a sheet over the sofa, add a pillow, then exit.)*

(While this happens, **ELODIE** *comes downstage with a glass of wine, looks out the window into the street, takes a long drink, finishes what's left in the glass, leaves it on the table, then exits.)*

(Just before **ELODIE** *exits,* **MOLLY** *enters with her toiletry bag, sits on the sofa, and reads. From down the hall, we see light coming from under a door, and hear the offstage voices of* **MARCELLE** *and* **CHARLES** *having a heated discussion. We cannot make out the words:)*

CHARLES. *(Offstage.)* What do you want me to say? What?

MARCELLE. *(Offstage.)* Twice is not an accident. Twice is not bad luck. Twice is insane.

CHARLES. *(Offstage.)* So our son's insane. So he's insane. So then what? What do you want to do? Badger the boy into submission? It's not gonna work! It's not Marcelle, so –

MARCELLE. *(Offstage.)* Shhh, enough!

(With that, **MARCELLE** *and* **CHARLES** *are quiet. During this fight,* **DANIEL** *enters to listen, wearing pajama pants. No more blood on his face, though he moves tentatively. He forgot* **MOLLY** *was there.)*

DANIEL. Excuse me.

MOLLY. Oh it's OK.

DANIEL. I was just, getting some water. I didn't mean to disturb you.

MOLLY. You're not. I'm just, reading.

(**DANIEL** *tries to look.*)

It's... embarrassing.

DANIEL. Ernest Hemingway? Why is that embarrassing?

MOLLY. For an American, to come to Paris and read *A Moveable Feast*? It's a cliché.

DANIEL. Uh, don't, uh – Don't tell?

MOLLY. Don't tell?

DANIEL. That I was, just now, uhm... standing, listening.

MOLLY. Oh, I won't. I do that, too, when my parents are fighting. Or, talking. I didn't mean to say your parents were...

DANIEL. I think it's universal.

MOLLY. Yeah.

(*Quick beat.*)

Does it hurt?

DANIEL. A little. But don't tell my mother?

MOLLY. Maybe – do you have, uhm, a steak or something?

DANIEL. A steak?

MOLLY. Isn't that what they do in movies? After a fight?

DANIEL. Oh yeah! I've seen that in movies.

MOLLY. Right?

DANIEL. Does it work?

MOLLY. It works in movies.

DANIEL. I'm OK.

MOLLY. It's happened before, to you?

DANIEL. Not like this.

MOLLY. But it's happened?

(**DANIEL** *shrugs.*)

What was the –

DANIEL. So you're here for a year?

MOLLY. What? Oh, yeah.

DANIEL. To learn French?

MOLLY. I know French, I –

DANIEL. Yes, you speak well.

MOLLY. Thank you. But I want to get better.

DANIEL. Why?

MOLLY. I don't know. I also… wanted to leave school for a while?

I kind of had a uh, a pretty bad break up last semester? And I needed some, uhm, distance.

DANIEL. Oh.

He sounds like a real jerk.

MOLLY. Oh, no he…

DANIEL. He must be a real –

MOLLY. No. It was a she.

DANIEL. Oh.

(*Beat.*)

MOLLY. I'm sorry, that's totally a lie, I don't know why I said that. It's a he, it's definitely a he.

DANIEL. OK.

MOLLY. I just... I'm not the kind of person who, who makes decisions because some guy broke my heart, but then I made this big decision because some guy broke my heart and I'm kind of embarrassed. By myself – can I start over? I came to France because I wanted to learn French.

DANIEL. So you're not a lesbian?

MOLLY. No. No. Not that – I mean, if I met the right girl, I try to be openminded...

DANIEL. So you're maybe a lesbian?

MOLLY. Sorry. I need to just – no. I am not a lesbian.

DANIEL. I'm gonna get some water.

MOLLY. Uh huh.

> (**DANIEL** *exits into the kitchen.* **MOLLY** *could not hate herself more than she does at this moment.)*

> (**DANIEL** *returns with two glasses, and hands one to* **MOLLY**.*)*

Oh. Thank you.

DANIEL. You're welcome.

MOLLY. Thanks.

> (**DANIEL** *isn't going anywhere, it seems. He takes a sip of his water. Unsure of what to do,* **MOLLY** *takes a sip of hers. He stands before her, while she sits on the couch, drinking the water.* **DANIEL** *seems less uncomfortable with the silence.* **MOLLY** *searches for something to say.)*

It's so nice of your parents, to host me. And your sister seems... sweet.

DANIEL. Well she's very brilliant. She's a very brilliant person.

MOLLY. How long have you two lived here?

DANIEL. In this apartment? Our whole lives.

MOLLY. Oh wow, so you never – you always lived with your parents?

DANIEL. Oh, no. I left for school, but when I started teaching in Sarcelles, my parents didn't want me to live there, but I couldn't afford my own place here, so –

MOLLY. Why didn't they want you to live in...

DANIEL. They thought it was dangerous.

MOLLY. Is it?

DANIEL. It's OK. You know, some people moved away, but, that's their choice.

MOLLY. Why did they move?

DANIEL. It's complicated.

MOLLY. What happened?

DANIEL. Well. There's been, you know, attacks before and, but then last year, maybe you heard about the shooting at Charlie Hebdo, the newspaper? And then they went to this kosher supermarket in Paris and killed four Jews who were, just shopping for groceries. So the people took to the streets to march for peace, millions of people. But Netanyahu came and told all the Jews to come to Israel, but then Manuel Valls got up and he said –

MOLLY. Who?

DANIEL. Our Prime Minister, Manuel Valls, he said something like, if 100,000 Frenchmen of Spanish origin left, France would still be France but if 100,000 French Jews left, France would no longer be France. The French Republic would be judged a failure. And, I mean, 100,000 Jews definitely did not leave last year, only around 8,000? Which is the most in a single year to leave France in a long time. So. It's a thing. But some of the people who moved away were teachers, so the school needs teachers cause the kids can't really go to public school anymore, but... and I like the students. They're really cool.

MOLLY. What do you teach?

DANIEL. Can't you tell?

MOLLY. Uhm, I don't know. Jewish stuff?

DANIEL. No. It's – it's a Jewish school, everyone is Jewish.

MOLLY. Oh.

DANIEL. Math. I teach math.

MOLLY. Really?

DANIEL. Yes, why, do I not seem geeky enough to be a math teacher?

MOLLY. No, you do, it's just –

DANIEL. Oh. So I'm geeky? Thank you.

MOLLY. Sorry. I didn't mean it like that.

DANIEL. I'm just teasing.

MOLLY. Oh. OK.

How, how did you get to be so religious?

DANIEL. I'm not so religious.

MOLLY. I mean, you teach in a Jewish school, you wear...

> (**MOLLY** *indicates his kippah.*)

DANIEL. Uh huh.

MOLLY. It's... interesting. To me.

DANIEL. *(Laughing.)* OK.

MOLLY. What?

DANIEL. Nothing.

MOLLY. What? Why are you, laughing at me?

DANIEL. I'm not.

MOLLY. You are.

DANIEL. Look, I really respect you Molly, I do. But I can tell you think I'm, uh, pretty ridiculous, actually, to say the least, so –

MOLLY. I never said you were ridiculous!

DANIEL. But I can tell that's what you think, so –

MOLLY. You have no idea what I think.

DANIEL. OK.

MOLLY. You don't, you don't even know me. You have no idea how I feel.

DANIEL. Then how do you feel?

MOLLY. You have no idea. And you have no right to assume...

DANIEL. So tell me: how do you feel?

MOLLY. About what?

DANIEL. About people like me. About religious Jews. About Jews.

MOLLY. I feel... Don't turn this around on me, I was asking *you* –

DANIEL. OK.

MOLLY. Because I'm, I'm *of* Jewish extraction, OK, so I don't –

DANIEL. Of Jewish extraction. Wow.

MOLLY. I am.

DANIEL. No, I – I believe you it's just, such a disdainful way of referring to yourself but –

MOLLY. Excuse me?

DANIEL. I said, it's a disdainful way of referring to yourself.

MOLLY. It's not. It's accurate.

DANIEL. Right. OK.

Hey, I'm gonna go to bed now.

MOLLY. Did I – are you upset?

DANIEL. Yeah. A little. Yeah.

MOLLY. OK... I don't – OK.

DANIEL. I – I actually have a fair amount of, uh, experience with people like you, in my life.

MOLLY. Oh do you?

DANIEL. I do. And in my experience, people who say things like, *of* Jewish extraction, are actually *more* dogmatic about religion than religious people, so I try to avoid the subject with those who clearly have disdain for – me.

MOLLY. Uhm. Wow. OK. Well, I'd say it sounds like you actually have disdain for me, but...

DANIEL. I don't.

MOLLY. Well that's not how it sounds to me.

DANIEL. OK.

MOLLY. OK. Well. Good night, Daniel.

(*Beat.*)

DANIEL. I upset you.

MOLLY. Yes. You did.

DANIEL. I apologize.

MOLLY. OK.

DANIEL. That was not my intention. I apologize. Genuinely.

MOLLY. Maybe, you know, maybe it's people like you who've made it impossible for me to feel proud of who I am.

DANIEL. Maybe it is.

MOLLY. It's people like you who take territory that isn't yours –

DANIEL. I haven't taken any territory –

MOLLY. And build settlements –

DANIEL. Molly –

MOLLY. And force people off land that is rightfully –

DANIEL. Molly!

MOLLY. What?

DANIEL. I don't want to talk about Israel.

MOLLY. OK. Then why are you standing here.

DANIEL. I was just trying to get to know you.

MOLLY. And I was trying to get to know you. I came to you, very genuinely, with an open – and then you turned it around and made all these assumptions when you don't, you don't even know me.

DANIEL. I'm sorry.

MOLLY. I was just asking how you became religious. That was all I wanted to know. If you didn't want to tell me, you don't have to, but you don't have to be, uhm…

DANIEL. I'm sorry.

MOLLY. OK.

    (Beat.)

DANIEL. I guess it was a few years ago now, there was one winter, it didn't snow. It just did not snow. And people kept talking about climate change and global warming, so it was on my mind, but also, I love winter. And to be in Paris when it snows... it doesn't get old, at least, not to me. But this one winter, no snow. December, January, February. Nothing. Finally, it's the first week of March, I'm walking to the metro... I feel flurries. It was too warm for anything to stick, but still – flurries. And I felt... grateful: to be alive, to have grown up at a time when I really got to experience winter. I wanted to say thank you, but who do you thank for the snow? So I went to synagogue, and I prayed, and, I liked it, so I kept going. And I'm – I'm still figuring out how I feel about, you know, God but, I believe in the Earth. That feels close enough.

> *(A beat. They are both thinking about kissing the other person, but unsure if that's unseemly.)*

You think I'm ridiculous?

MOLLY. No. I don't.

DANIEL. *(Laughing.)* I feel a little ridiculous. Talking about the snow, and –

MOLLY. Well you shouldn't.

DANIEL. I shouldn't?

MOLLY. No. It's actually... *(Unspoken: lovely.)*

> *(They're now much closer to kissing, and that's just the moment* **CHARLES** *walks into the living room.* **MOLLY** *and* **DANIEL** *turn away from each other, as if they've been caught doing something wrong.* **CHARLES** *immediately reads the situation correctly but acts like there's no tension in the room.)*

DANIEL. Oh. I was just getting... water.

CHARLES. OK. How are you feeling?

DANIEL. I'm OK.

CHARLES. OK. I'll, I'll take a look in the morning.

DANIEL. OK. Thanks.

CHARLES. Yep.

(**CHARLES** *exits into the kitchen.*)

DANIEL. You must be tired.

MOLLY. Yeah.

DANIEL. OK, well, have a good – water.

(**DANIEL** *exits.* **MOLLY** *turns out the light.*)

(*In the dark, we hear a* **MALE VOICE** *say:*)

MALE VOICE. And now, we rise to recite the Prayer for the French Republic.

(*The offstage* **COMPANY**, *in unison, should join the* **MALE VOICE** *for each "Amen."*)

(*Perhaps we see* **CHARLES** *and* **DANIEL** *cross the stage, or* **CHARLES** *listening, taking the words in. Or perhaps we see something else. Or nothing.*)

O Lord, Master of the world, your Providence embraces the heavens and the earth, strength and power belong to you: by you alone, everything rises and everything grows stronger. From your holy dwelling, O Lord, bless and protect THE FRENCH REPUBLIC AND THE FRENCH PEOPLE. – Amen!

May France live happily and prosperously; may it be strong and great by union and harmony. – Amen!

MALE VOICE. May the rays of Your light enlighten those who preside over the destinies of our nation and cause order and justice to reign. – Amen!

May France enjoy a lasting peace and preserve her glorious rank among the nations. – Amen!

May France remain faithful to her noble Tradition and always defend law and freedom. – Amen!

Look favorably upon our vows; that the words of our lips and the feelings of our hearts find grace before you, O Lord, our creator and our deliverer. – Amen!

> *(Later that morning.)*

> *(***MARCELLE*** *enters, carrying some bread and croissants. She puts them on the table, then calls out:)*

MARCELLE. Elodie? It's time to get up.

ELODIE. *(Offstage.)* I'm sleeping.

MARCELLE. It's almost noon, we don't sleep all day.

Elodie.

Elodie!

ELODIE. *(Offstage.)* Five minutes!

MARCELLE. Five minutes. But then I want you up and out of bed, OK?

OK?

ELODIE. *(Offstage.)* Okayyyyyy!

> *(***MARCELLE*** *is about to set up breakfast when she notices the empty wine glass.)*

MARCELLE. Elodie? Is this your wine glass you left here?

Elodie?

ELODIE. *(Offstage.)* Stop!

MARCELLE. Do you have a personal maid I don't know about?

> (**ELODIE** *storms in, fresh from bed, in pajamas. She takes the wine glass into the kitchen, then returns without it.*)

ELODIE. Happy?

MARCELLE. So who has the honor now of putting it in the dishwasher? You leave it in the sink and now, what, the magic dishwashing fairy will take care of it? I work hard all week, while you lie around doing God knows what – Do I look like a magic dishwashing fairy to you?

> (*On "sink"* **ELODIE** *storms back to the kitchen, forcefully puts the wine glass in the dishwasher, then returns.*)

ELODIE. No. You look like a bitch.

MARCELLE. Yes I'm a bitch for not wanting to clean up after you.

ELODIE. I was gonna clean it up, relax! It was bothering you so much?

MARCELLE. Yes! It's my house! I like it neat, Farida is not here on the weekends, even if she were she's not your personal maid.

ELODIE. I cleaned it up can you not yell this early in the –

MARCELLE. Early? I already ran five kilometers! And shopped! Responded to fifty emails –

ELODIE. Can you not yell.

MARCELLE. You want to leave your wine glasses out all over the place, get your own apartment. You want to live in *my* home, clean up after yourself.

ELODIE. Got. It.

> (**ELODIE** *tries to exit.*)

MARCELLE. And you don't sleep the whole day away!

ELODIE. Oh my god what do you care?

MARCELLE. Because. We're not doing that anymore. We are not – you will sit down, I just got you some – and you will eat something.

ELODIE. I'm. Not. Hungry.

MARCELLE. I. Don't. Care.

ELODIE. I'm not hungry! I'm twenty-eight years old I know when I'm hungry, I'm not hungry!

MARCELLE. Then you will sit with Molly while she eats. Where is she?

ELODIE. How the fuck should I know?

MARCELLE. Elodie.

> (**MARCELLE** *walks a few steps toward the bathroom.*)

She's still in the bathroom.

ELODIE. OK.

MARCELLE. She was in the bathroom when I left.

ELODIE. Are you keeping tabs?

MARCELLE. No I'm not keeping tabs, thank you.

> (*A brand new tone, genuinely warm.*)

These are fresh, would you like one?

ELODIE. (*Still angry.*) No thank you.

MARCELLE. Elodie.

ELODIE. OK sure, thank you.

> (**MARCELLE** *puts a croissant on a plate, and motions for* **ELODIE** *to sit. She sits.* **MARCELLE** *sits too, then waits for* **ELODIE** *to eat.*)

MARCELLE. Your father walked in on Molly and your brother last night.

ELODIE. Uch! Really?

MARCELLE. Mmm hmmm.

ELODIE. Where?

MARCELLE. Right there.

ELODIE. Daniel had sex in our living room?

MARCELLE. What? No!

ELODIE. Then what...

MARCELLE. They were in there, in the dark. On the couch together.

ELODIE. What do you mean, together, like –

MARCELLE. On the couch. Sitting very close together.

ELODIE. Were they doing anything?

MARCELLE. I don't know.

ELODIE. Mom. When two people are sitting together, and somebody else enters the room, you don't say that they walked in on them. That's not, that's not how that works.

MARCELLE. You don't find it a little uncomfortable, this cousin you've never met, the first night she's here and suddenly she's putting the moves on your brother?

ELODIE. Was she putting the moves on him?

MARCELLE. I don't know. Maybe.

> (**ELODIE** *gives up with her mother. She puts her face in her hands, breathes deeply, then slides her hands down her face.*)

Sweetie?

ELODIE. Yes Mom.

MARCELLE. I need your help.

ELODIE. With what?

MARCELLE. Don't say it like that.

ELODIE. *(Fakely sweet.)* With what?

MARCELLE. Forget it.

ELODIE. What!

MARCELLE. Talk to your brother.

ELODIE. What am I supposed to do?

MARCELLE. He worships you.

ELODIE. Um, OK.

MARCELLE. Even just a baseball cap, something to cover his – if you could get him to – explain that, it's okay – in a dangerous world, self-preservation is not incidental –

ELODIE. You should just say something if you feel so strongly.

MARCELLE. I have. Believe me I have. You know I have. He doesn't listen. He would listen to you.

ELODIE. I doubt that.

MARCELLE. Will you at least – will you think about it? Elodie?

ELODIE. Yeah, I'll think about it.

MARCELLE. It would mean a lot to me.

ELODIE. OK.

MARCELLE. Aren't you hungry?

ELODIE. No.

MARCELLE. No?

ELODIE. No.

MARCELLE. But you had a lot to drink last night?

(**ELODIE** *wants to scream. Instead she starts laughing.*)

ELODIE. Mom. I had two glasses of wine.

MARCELLE. The bottle was empty.

ELODIE. Because there were five of us. We shared one bottle of wine. As a family. Eating dinner. What are you even talking about?

MARCELLE. I don't like you drinking.

ELODIE. I had two glasses of wine! I do not have a drinking problem! I had two –

MARCELLE. I didn't say you had a drinking problem, all I said –

ELODIE. Two. *With* dinner. Two glasses of wine does not make someone an alcoholic!

MARCELLE. I never said you were an alcoholic –

ELODIE. A manic depressive episode is not the same thing as alcoholism, I would think you of all people would know that –

MARCELLE. An episode doesn't last two years Elodie!

ELODIE. It can!

MARCELLE. When left untreated! When not properly treated! But when you drink all night and then sleep all day, that's not –

ELODIE. I HAD TWO GLASSES OF WINE! WITH DINNER! That does not qualify as drinking all night! When two people are talking, you don't say you walked in on them. And when a person has a glass of wine with dinner, you don't say they're an alcoholic.

MARCELLE. Not *a* glass. Two. Two. Two glasses.

ELODIE. OH MY GOD! You sound INSANE right now.

MARCELLE. Fine. I'm insane. You're right Elodie. You know what? Why don't you go back to bed. It's only noon, after all, you're missing out on at least another six good hours of sleep before –

(**MOLLY** *emerges from the bathroom, dressed, with her toiletry bag. She didn't wash her hair. She goes to her suitcase.*)

MOLLY. Excuse me.

(**MARCELLE** *stares at* **ELODIE**; *she is not in the mood to entertain some stranger right now. Even though she went out and bought croissants.* **MOLLY** *doesn't know what to do with herself. She wants to look busy, as she senses tension, but she really has nothing to put away or take out.*)

MARCELLE. Have you eaten?

MOLLY. Oh, no, not yet.

MARCELLE. We have bread, croissants, there's cereal...

MOLLY. Can I, could I have a croissant?

MARCELLE. Please. Why don't you join Elodie. She was just about to eat.

(**MOLLY** *comes to the table, takes a croissant, puts it on a plate.*)

MOLLY. They're warm.

MARCELLE. Yes, they're fresh.

(**MOLLY** *takes a bite.*)

MOLLY. Oh my Goooooood.

(*She chews very slowly, almost in disbelief.*)

Where did you get these?

MARCELLE. Down the street.

MOLLY. I love this country.

Sorry, I just, I have never had anything this, uhm, good before? In my entire life?

MARCELLE. *(To* **ELODIE**, *as if to say, if the croissants are that good, you should eat some, too.)* Well then.

> *(***ELODIE*** finally rips off a small piece of the croissant and eats it. She glares at* **MARCELLE**, *who exits down the hall to the bathroom.)*

(Offstage.) Elodie. I'm opening the window, in case you want to take a shower. It's all steamed up.

MOLLY. Oh. I'm sor– I'm sorry.

> *(***MOLLY*** walks toward the bathroom.)*

Is there anything I can...

MARCELLE. *(Offstage.)* No. I just opened the window.

MOLLY. I, I guess I was in there longer than I... I'm sorry.

> *(***MOLLY*** returns and tries to sit down noiselessly.)*

(Whispered.) I am so embarrassed.

> *(***ELODIE*** says nothing.)*

My French mother doesn't let me take long showers, so...

Do you think she's mad, that I was in the bathroom too long?

ELODIE. Yes.

MOLLY. Really?

ELODIE. Yes.

MOLLY. Oh.

(The front door opens. **CHARLES** *and* **DANIEL** *enter.)*

DANIEL. Hey.

MOLLY. Hi.

MARCELLE. *(Offstage.)* How were services?

DANIEL. Very nice.

MOLLY. Oh, you went to –

MARCELLE. *(Offstage.)* If you want lunch, help yourself but I just got some croissants –

DANIEL. OK, thanks.

MARCELLE. Charles? Are you hungry?

(**MARCELLE** *has returned.* **CHARLES** *doesn't respond.)*

Charles?

(**CHARLES** *shakes his head no.)*

Are you OK? Are you –

(Again, he shakes his head no.)

CHARLES. I think I – I need to sit.

MARCELLE. Charles?

CHARLES. I can't... I can't get oxygen.

ELODIE. Are you having a panic attack?

CHARLES. *(Nodding yes.)* I...

(**MARCELLE** *seats him in a chair.)*

MARCELLE. Breathe. Just breathe. In through your nose, out through your mouth. In through your nose. Out through your –

(She turns to **DANIEL**.*)*

What happened?

DANIEL. Nothing. We were just walking. He was quiet, but –

CHARLES. I can't do this anymore.

MARCELLE. Just breathe.

CHARLES. I can't, I can't do this anymore.

MARCELLE. Do what, honey?

CHARLES. Live. Here. I can't live here anymore. I can't do it.

MARCELLE. What? Oh. OK well this can wait.

CHARLES. I'm done waiting.

MARCELLE. Just breathe. Just –

CHARLES. I want to move.

MARCELLE. In through your nose –

CHARLES. I want to move.

MARCELLE. Charles I'm not really in the mood for this again –

ELODIE. Mom, he's trying to express something. Don't shut him down.

CHARLES. You're never in the mood, but now, I'm in the mood.

MARCELLE. You want to move?

CHARLES. I want to move.

MARCELLE. And where would you like to go?

CHARLES. Israel.

MARCELLE. Israel.

CHARLES. Yes.

MARCELLE. OK. Great choice. Do you speak Hebrew?

CHARLES. I'll learn.

MARCELLE. You'll learn. Sounds easy. Do you have a job lined up?

ELODIE. You don't have to be so snotty –

CHARLES. I'll find one.

MARCELLE. What luck! A new job in a foreign language –

ELODIE. Mom!

CHARLES. I can't do this anymore. OK? I cannot – I walked beside our son this morning, all the way to synagogue… the looks he got, the way some people looked at him –

MARCELLE. And we have been over this, a thousand times. If he did not, so overtly, display his religious identity, this would not be a problem –

DANIEL. I don't want to wear some stupid baseball cap –

MARCELLE. Yes God forbid you take any precautions –

CHARLES. It's not about a baseball cap, Marcelle. The issue is not how Daniel dresses, don't you see? He could cover up, he could never leave the house again, it wouldn't change the fact that this is how people feel. We know it. We know it because when given the chance, they express it. Our son's been attacked twice now. He can't walk down the street without people staring at him, glaring at him, menacingly –

MARCELLE. Maybe they were staring because his face is swollen. Did you think about that?

CHARLES. I don't think that's the case –

MARCELLE. Because if I saw that on the street, I'd stare too.

ELODIE. Mom! Listen to what Dad is saying! Can you just listen?

CHARLES. I walked with my son, down the streets of Paris, to synagogue. And I saw the faces. And then we sat, and prayed. They read the Torah, they read the Haftorah, and then the Rabbi asked us to rise, so we could say the Prayer for the French Republic. A prayer which I have said – how many times? But it never hit me – until today, the weight of it. Every week they say it, every week for two hundred years, through Dreyfus, through Vichy, every generation, even when... and frankly, I'm tired of praying for someone else to protect me. I'm tired of it. And, to be totally honest, I don't think it's working –

MARCELLE. That's because you don't believe in praying, you don't believe in God, what are you talking about –

CHARLES. I'm talking about the prayer I said this morning.

MARCELLE. Since when do you put stock in prayers?

CHARLES. That's what I'm saying! They're – they're stabbing Jews in Strasbourg. They're stabbing Jews in Marseille. They're –

MARCELLE. Uh, they're stabbing Jews in Israel, too.

CHARLES. Yes but in Israel, our son could walk down the street, in Haifa, in Tel Aviv, and not fear for his life.

DANIEL. I don't fear for my life.

CHARLES. Well I do! I'm tired of seeing armed guards outside every school, every synagogue – carrying machine guns – MACHINE GUNS!?! Why are we not safe here? Why are we in danger?

MARCELLE. So your solution is to move to Israel? Honey, do you need me to buy you a newspaper? You feel unsafe, so you want to move to Israel?

CHARLES. At least in Israel, we're all unsafe. We're equally unsafe.

MARCELLE. I think we're pretty equally unsafe right here in Paris. Did you forget about the Bataclan? About –

CHARLES. No I did not forget about the Bataclan, but, it's not the same, the – the terrorists may hate the French, but they hate us most of all. And they hate us on the right, and they hate us on the left. They hate us here.

MARCELLE. News flash: they hate us everywhere. They don't hate us less in other countries, in fact –

CHARLES. And it's getting worse. The writing is on the wall – I. Can't. Do it anymore. I can't. I want to move to Israel.

MARCELLE. OK. Well, I don't.

CHARLES. I, I... you're not hearing me.

MARCELLE. What am I not hearing?

CHARLES. I won't live here anymore. I am moving to Israel. I want *us* to move to Israel.

MOLLY. Uhmmm.

I would just say uhm... before you make any decisions, if I could maybe share some information, or articles, because – I know it can be sensitive, words get tossed around which isn't always helpful – settlements, and human rights violations, and uhm, I'm not sure what the word is in French, maybe it's the same – apartheid? But when you *listen* to the *stories*, of what's *happening* over there, it can change how you think about things, I know it did for me, so. I'm just putting that out there. In case that's helpful.

> *(Beat.)*

ELODIE. Yes that's very helpful. Thank you Molly.

MOLLY. Sure.

ELODIE. I had no *idea* Israel's occupation of Palestine was so problematic. Thank you so much for that.

MOLLY. OK.

ELODIE. Did you guys have any idea Israel was such a problematic nation?

DANIEL. Elodie.

ELODIE. I'm curious, how'd you come to learn so much about this?

DANIEL. OK, OK, enough.

ELODIE. I'm just asking a question.

MOLLY. I, I educated myself. I read.

ELODIE. You read.

MOLLY. I read.

ELODIE. Books, articles?

MOLLY. Yes.

CHARLES. Let's quit while we're ahead, shall we?

ELODIE. No it's just so interesting to me because I'm also a student of history, I'm curious.

MARCELLE. You're not curious.

ELODIE. Did you happen to read said articles on your laptop?

CHARLES.	**MARCELLE.**
You made your point. You made your point.	Oh no. No laptop today. No laptop.

ELODIE.	
Because as I'm sure you already know, laptops are full of *coltan*, the mining of which has wreaked utter devastation on African environments.	If I have to hear about coltan one more time, no one cares about coltan!

ELODIE. That's the problem! We don't care who has to DIE so we can play Candy Crush! Which is just like Molly!

DANIEL. You own a phone! You own a laptop!

ELODIE. No I'm just trying to understand, when you first learned about Israeli occupation, were you in your little pink bedroom on the Upper East Side?

MOLLY. If, if you're asking if I am aware of the flaws, the major flaws of my own country: yes, I'm very aware.

ELODIE. You're aware! She's aware! We can all relax, she's aware!

MOLLY. And I don't disagree, the history of America is, horrifying, but it's not –

ELODIE. But it's not so awful that you plan to *do* anything about it. Midtown Manhattan is not your motherland, yet you feel totally justified sitting on *your stolen* land, educating yourself about human rights violations on *your* phone made of *stolen* minerals, dug by slave labor, and then standing up with no irony whatsoever and saying: "I Decry Occupation!" I mean... *So Brave.*

CHARLES. I think you've made your point.

ELODIE. Or are you *actually* concerned with occupation, cause, you know you could start by leaving YOUR occupied lands?

MARCELLE. Why don't *you* leave? I'm so sorry Molly.

MOLLY. But, all countries have done wrong. America. Uhm. Germany...

ELODIE. Uh huh...

MOLLY. And, and Israel also needs to be held to, you know, the –

ELODIE. There it is! I was *wondering* how long I'd have to wait for the Israeli–Nazi comparisons, but it's right on time!

CHARLES. You made your point!

ELODIE. No I've had it with this shit. I will not be lectured to about what we should do, so we feel safe, by someone who gets to sleep as soundly as she does every night in her bedroom built over a pile of other people's BLOOD and GUTS. And I will not just sit here, mealy mouthed while she's just *putting it out there* for us, like we're morons, when she's got more blood on her hands than anyone.

DANIEL. She does not have blood on her hands!

ELODIE. Look at those bloody fucking hands! And you're still living on the Upper East Side, aren't you? Aren't you! Aren't you!

MARCELLE. Molly, I'm so sorry, Elodie suffers from manic depression.

ELODIE. Oh thanks Mom! Yes, Molly, this is gonna shock you but I have a mental health problem. I'm sure you had *no* idea there was anything wrong with me.

MARCELLE. Elodie go to your room.

ELODIE. I'm not seven.

MOLLY. No it's – I actually wanted to see some museums today, so –

MARCELLE. You do not need to go –

MOLLY. No it's totally fine, I'll be back, uhm –

DANIEL. Molly –

MOLLY. I'll be back later.

DANIEL. You really don't have to go. Molly.

MOLLY. No, it's OK, it's OK. This is what happens. All I did was try to point out some injustice *might* be taking place, and your immediate response is to deflect, and call me a hypocrite. Just for speaking. What are you so afraid of?

*(As **MOLLY** exits, and **DANIEL** follows her out:)*

ELODIE. Don't talk to me about injustice, I'm the Queen of standing up against injustice! The queen!

MARCELLE. Yeah, you're the queen alright.

ELODIE. All I do is stand up against injustice!

MARCELLE. Where? In your bed? On your computer? To your five little friends no one cares about?

ELODIE. I will never understand how you are a person people seek for compassionate treatment.

MARCELLE. Elodie you have said enough for one day, OK? You've used up your word count.

ELODIE. You don't get to dictate my word count –

CHARLES. Your mother's right. It's enough out of you.

ELODIE. Jesus Christ!

*(**DANIEL** returns.)*

MARCELLE. Is Molly OK?

DANIEL. Uh, not really. You really, uh, did not need to take it that far.

ELODIE. Oh I'm sorry, were you enjoying that guest lecture on Israeli policy?

DANIEL. That's not the point, she's a guest and now she's...

ELODIE. I don't know, when my guests start saying –

MARCELLE. Elodie! Elodie! Enough.

ELODIE. Fine.

Mom thinks you fucked	
Molly in the living room	**MARCELLE**.
last night, although even	Elodie! Elodie!
if you did I think after	Enough!
that anti-Zionist display	I never said that.

the rose is off that bloom, also Mom says you worship me so I should tell you to wear a baseball cap but personally I think you should dress however the fuck you want.

MARCELLE. Thank you Elodie.

DANIEL. For the love of God will everyone please stop telling me how to dress!

MARCELLE. Charles. Do something.

CHARLES. I am. I did.

MARCELLE. What?

CHARLES. I want to move to Israel, I said –

MARCELLE. I meant do something now, here, now.

CHARLES. That's what I'm trying to do!

MARCELLE. Very good, well I'm done talking about Israel for today.

CHARLES. Well I'm not.

ELODIE. Why are people in this family only allowed to talk if you agree with what they have to say?

CHARLES. Can I just –

MARCELLE. I'm done responding to you.

ELODIE. You silence anyone who isn't saying something you want to hear –

MARCELLE. Everyone ignore Elodie!

CHARLES. Can I –

CHARLES. I'm trying to speak!!!

ELODIE. Dad is trying to speak.

MARCELLE. So who's stopping you?

CHARLES & ELODIE. You!

MARCELLE. Well I can't listen to more of your, I walked down the street, I heard a prayer, I want to leave. I can't listen to that, OK? Our lives are here. They're here. We live here. You have a practice, I run a department. We have a home. Our children live here. All our friends. My father – and his needs are only growing, and we all know my brother is never going to step up and take responsibility for the overseeing of his care, which means, I need to be here. So let's say you decided, in a burst of romanticism, that you had to live by the sea, and we should move to Normandy, or Biarritz, or Antibes – we couldn't do it. We're too young to retire and we're too old to start over, even in our own country. We have too many obligations. So it's not just impractical, it's impossible, and frankly –

CHARLES. I'm scared.

> *(Beat.)*

I'm scared, Marcelle. You lay everything out, you lay it out so rationally, and I hear every word you're saying, but, I'm scared. We are Jews. We are Jews. The only reason we're still on this planet is because we learned to get out of dangerous situations before they got the better of us. Something is happening in the world, and it's happening in our country, too – I can feel it. I feel it when I walk with Daniel, I feel it when I read the left wing editorials, I feel it watching Le Pen and her base, all stirred up. Something is happening, and when that thing comes, I don't want to have to pray so my own country will protect me from it.

> *(On the other side of the stage, **IRMA** runs on, carrying a letter.)*

IRMA. Adolphe! Adolphe! My god, Adolphe!

CHARLES. Is it rational? Maybe not.

IRMA. Adolphe?

CHARLES. Is it practical? Absolutely not.

IRMA. Adolphe!

(**ADOLPHE** *enters.*)

ADOLPHE. What is it? What?

CHARLES. But my heart –

IRMA. It's news.

CHARLES. My gut.

IRMA. Lucien!

CHARLES. Every bone in my body, every inch of my core –

IRMA. And Pierre!

CHARLES. Is telling me the same thing:

MARCELLE. And what is that?

IRMA. They're coming home!

(*Beat.*)

CHARLES. Run.

(*Blackout.*)

ACT TWO

(**PATRICK** *enters, sits at the piano and begins to play "I Thought About You," the Jimmy Van Heusen/Johnny Mercer song. He sings:**)

PATRICK.
I TOOK A TRIP ON A TRAIN
AND I THOUGHT ABOUT YOU
I PASSED A SHADOWY LANE
AND I THOUGHT ABOUT YOU
TWO OR THREE CARS PARKED UNDER THE STARS
WINDING STREAM
MOON SHINING DOWN ON SOME LITTLE TOWN
AND WITH EACH BEAM, THE SAME OLD DREAM ...

(*He stops and turns to us.*)

Let's talk about the Crusades, shall we?

Jews are living in France for centuries when – in 1096 – the People's Crusade rolls into town. This is before the official Crusades, which were led by the Catholic church. This one was just for the people. Estimates vary, but they managed to kill about a third of France's Jews, so, not too shabby! Now. The People's Crusade was led by someone named Peter the Hermit. He was nice. He and his buddies would come to town, do some torturing, a little dragging around, a little killing, then pile the bodies up until they couldn't pile them any higher, and

---

* A license to produce *Prayer for the French Republic* includes permission to perform "I Thought About You," subject to a mandatory music fee. Please refer to your licensing agreement for important billing and credit requirements.

let me tell you, when you get to the point where you can't pile anymore dead bodies up, you've made some pretty impressive piles! But to be fair, a lot of Jews committed suicide to avoid being killed, so technically you can't blame Peter the Hermit for everything.

We know about this because someone wrote it down. A Jew whose name has been lost to history wrote something called the Mainz Anonymous. That's the thing about Jews, we write it all down. Look, if we didn't keep track of it, you think they'd keep track of it for us?

The Mainz Anonymous is a great read, I have to say, I highly recommend it. Here's how someone named Isaac son of Daniel died:

"They put a rope around his neck and dragged him through the entire city in the muddy streets to the house of their idolatry. There was still some life in his frame when they said to him: 'You can still be saved if you agree to change your religion.' Having already been strangled, he could not utter a word from his mouth, so he gestured with his finger to say: 'Cut off my head.' And they slit his throat."

Sorry, was that too much? I forget what it's like, the first time you hear the details…

    (**PATRICK** *returns to the piano.*)

I TOOK A TRIP ON A TRAIN
AND I THOUGHT ABOUT YOU
I PASSED A SHADOWY LANE
AND I THOUGHT ABOUT YOU

Truth be told, I didn't know all this growing up. Mom wasn't Jewish, Dad wasn't religious. Other than weddings and funerals, we didn't do too much with religion. We just wanted to be French. And we are! But then Marcelle married who she married, their children became who they became, and every year they got a little more…

(He makes some gesture to suggest whatever they've become, he thinks it's too much.)

I mean, the idea that France isn't safe? France! The first country in Europe to emancipate its Jews? The country our family loved so much that, in 1870 when Germany annexed the region where they had lived for centuries, they moved! Went west, to remain French, that's how much they loved it and it must have broken their hearts – because Strasbourg is fucking gorgeous. I was there on business actually, not too long ago. Gorgeous. Cobblestone streets, nice shopping – I had a little time to kill before my train back to Paris, so I was strolling around, buying a couple things, before you know it, I'm on Jew Street – which I assure you is a totally benign name you see in lots of cities here that means, "Street where Jews live – lived," and out of the corner of my eye, I see a faded stone plaque on the side of a building: "In this section was the center of the medieval Jewish community, prior to the massacre of 1349."

Who knew? Turns out 2,000 people were killed – burned alive – during what's affectionately known as the Valentine's Day massacre, cause they were a little more humane that day, they spared the children. And also women they found attractive, so, that's something.

(He pauses, still looking at the plaque.)

Do I descend from survivors of this massacre? My family lived in this area for centuries, they spared the attractive women and, well, look at us: we're gorgeous. But no one ever talked about it. What would they have said?

It was the middle of the night. She was a pretty young mother. She held her tiny baby to her breast as she watched her husband being burned alive. She thought she could make out his scream but so many were screaming, it was hard to know which was his, and to be fair, she'd never heard him make a sound like that before.

Who wants to hear *that* story. So they didn't talk about it. Or maybe they talked about it for a while, then something else horrible happened, and it was forgotten. That's how history works.

I mean, what is history, but a bunch of stuff other people tell you to get over already? So you do. You stop remembering. And eventually, everyone forgets. Even when you write it down, they forget! Or maybe they want to forget. Or maybe they *need* to forget, just to put one foot in front of the other.

> (**LUCIEN** *emerges on the other side of the stage.*)

AT EVERY STOP THAT WE MADE
OH I THOUGHT ABOUT YOU
BUT WHEN I PULLED DOWN THE SHADE
THEN I REALLY FELT BLUE

> (*Lights fade on* **PATRICK**, *he disappears into the dark, but the music continues, switching from something live to something canned. Suddenly it's an old version of the song, from the 1940s, coming through a radio in Irma and Adolphe's living room.*)

> (**LUCIEN** *stands, rapt, listening, taking it all in.*)

> (*We are alone with him for a long moment.*)

> (**IRMA** *enters, drying her hands on a dishtowel.*)

IRMA. I really didn't recognize you.

I've never seen you so thin in my life, Lucien.

> (*Beat.*)

LUCIEN. You got the radio back.

IRMA. Sure, in August? Whenever they left. Where's Pierre?

LUCIEN. Taking a bath.

IRMA. Still?

LUCIEN. He's fifteen mother. He's got a lot to, figure out.

IRMA. I guess that's true.

　　You had enough to eat?

LUCIEN. What? Yeah. Dinner was good, thanks.

IRMA. OK. Only – you used to eat much more.

LUCIEN. Well, I used to be fat.

IRMA. You were never fat.

　　A healthy eater.

LUCIEN. How diplomatic.

IRMA. It's been a long time since I had more than two
　　dishes to wash...

LUCIEN. Do you have today's paper?

IRMA. Maybe. Who knows?

LUCIEN. Or a recent one? Anything?

IRMA. I'm sure we do, somewhere. I'm afraid we've become
　　those people.

LUCIEN. What people?

IRMA. People with piles of crap everywhere.

LUCIEN. *Become?*

　　　　(**IRMA** *and* **LUCIEN** *look for a paper.*)

IRMA. You saw the postcard? From Jacqueline? They're in
　　Mexico now. From Cuba to Mexico.

LUCIEN. The grand tour...

IRMA. They met Hemingway. Or saw him, in Havana.

LUCIEN. Good for them.

(Beat.)

IRMA. I thought about you every day, Lucien. I prayed for you. I never prayed in my life, but I prayed for you, every night. Ask your father.

LUCIEN. I believe you.

IRMA. Every night I prayed.

LUCIEN. Thank you.

IRMA. We didn't know where you were...

*(Beat. **IRMA** waits, expectantly, for **LUCIEN** to begin talking. He does not.)*

Where were you?

LUCIEN. Mom: You have to organize this table, it's...

IRMA. This morning, I know – you were in Strasbourg?

LUCIEN. Yes. A beautiful city.

IRMA. And, but – before Strasbourg, you were...

LUCIEN. I didn't realize how many canals they have.

IRMA. Where were you?

LUCIEN. You must have a newspaper.

IRMA. You can talk to me.

LUCIEN. Because this is...

IRMA. I'm your mother, Lucien, what happened?

LUCIEN. *(Extremely angry and intense.)* How do you find anything on this FUCKING TABLE!

*(**IRMA** is momentarily stunned. **LUCIEN** was not expecting to yell either. A long beat. Then **YOUNG PIERRE** enters, followed by **ADOLPHE**.)*

IRMA. Pierre.

ADOLPHE. Irma – the pajamas fit him fine.

IRMA. I – yes but, what about the shoes?

ADOLPHE. No, those were no good.

YOUNG PIERRE. They were OK.

ADOLPHE. His feet are bigger than mine, now.

LUCIEN. I told you to stop growing.

IRMA. He needs shoes that fit, he can't walk around... Add
that to the list.

> (**LUCIEN** *has collected himself.* **YOUNG PIERRE**
> *goes to his* **FATHER**, *casually, but drawn like
> a magnet. They don't touch. He just wants to
> be near him.)*

ADOLPHE. Would you like to play something for us?

IRMA. He just bathed.

ADOLPHE. So? You remember how to play. You always
played so nicely.

IRMA. Leave him be. You want to sit, darling? You've had
such a long day.

LUCIEN. Let's sit.

ADOLPHE. What did you think of my hometown? I was
born in Strasbourg, you know?

YOUNG PIERRE. It looked nice.

ADOLPHE. It is. I'll take you sometime, I'll show you where
my grandfather opened the first store...

> (*A very long, awkward beat.*)

> (*These four individuals have never been
> together in this particular configuration. It
> is not cold, but new, and uncertain. No one
> knows what to say.*)

IRMA. So. We need to get you shoes. And, clothes, you've grown so much. We have to call the doctor, I want him to look at you, both of you – and there's nothing in the house for breakfast, we have to get some food. Tell me, what would you like?

(**YOUNG PIERRE** *shrugs.*)

There has to be something, something you missed, maybe?

No?

LUCIEN. Tell Grandma. She wants to get you something nice.

(**LUCIEN** *smiles at his* **MOTHER.** *She's grateful.*)

YOUNG PIERRE. A croissant.

IRMA. A croissant. Oh. I don't, uhm…

ADOLPHE. We haven't had croissants since, before the war.

IRMA. Oh.

ADOLPHE. Rations.

LUCIEN. That's alright.

IRMA. I could get some bread though? In the morning. And butter? Would you like that?

(**YOUNG PIERRE** *nods.*)

I – I wish I could get you a croissant, only…

LUCIEN. Bread is great. That'll be great. Right pal? This is great.

(*The lights fade on them, and come up on that little boy's grown children, as* **PATRICK** *sits with his sister* **MARCELLE** *in her home.*)

PATRICK. That is the craziest thing I have ever heard.

MARCELLE. I know.

PATRICK. That is the craziest thing I have ever heard.

MARCELLE. You said that.

PATRICK. I can't believe he's – Have you ever even been to Israel?

MARCELLE. Once, maybe ten years ago, we took the kids.

PATRICK. And?

MARCELLE. It was OK, it was interesting.

PATRICK. That is the craziest thing I have ever heard.

MARCELLE. OK that's not helpful anymore.

PATRICK. So Charles is there now?

MARCELLE. Yes.

PATRICK. With Daniel?

MARCELLE. Of course with Daniel. You think he'd miss a chance to visit the holy land?

PATRICK. And Elodie?

MARCELLE. Elodie had a… she was supposed to go, who knows with her.

PATRICK. You're a psychiatrist, you would know.

MARCELLE. You would think.

PATRICK. I can't believe they went to – for how long?

MARCELLE. A few days.

PATRICK. But what are they even doing?

MARCELLE. Checking things out, looking around, I don't know. Seeing apartments.

PATRICK. Oh my god.

MARCELLE. He wants to leave before the election.

PATRICK. Oh come on! She's never going to win.

MARCELLE. You think I haven't been telling him that for months? But now that America elected –

PATRICK. But Americans are idiots.

MARCELLE. The most powerful nation on Earth…

PATRICK. Idiots. We have our issues but, France will never elect Le Pen, it will never happen, never.

MARCELLE. Can I get that in writing?

PATRICK. It will never happen.

MARCELLE. Charles says once he has an offer, he'll announce he's leaving the practice –

PATRICK. He's serious?

MARCELLE. He's in fucking Israel looking at apartments, I think he's serious.

PATRICK. But he spent the last thirty years building that practice.

MARCELLE. And his partners said they would buy him out.

PATRICK. But, I mean, you can't rebuild a practice it took you thirty years to build, overnight, in a new country –

MARCELLE. You think you're telling me something I haven't told him, a hundred times –

PATRICK. And you're just going to let him?

MARCELLE. He's a grown man, I can't stop him.

PATRICK. But what about you?

MARCELLE. What about me?

PATRICK. I mean, you didn't go with him.

MARCELLE. Correct, I am here, talking to you, in front of you, so –

PATRICK. Then, what's going to happen?

MARCELLE. I don't know, I guess he and Daniel will find a place in Israel, I don't know.

PATRICK. So you're, you're talking about divorce?

MARCELLE. Oh. No. It hasn't gotten there yet. He still thinks he can convince me to go.

PATRICK. But you would never. You would never! Would you ever?

MARCELLE. No.

PATRICK. You can't go. You – what would you do in Israel? We're French. We're – And you're the most French person I know. Look at you! You, in a desert?!? *You?*

MARCELLE. I don't even like going to the beach, Patrick, not even for a visit. Why would I want to *live* at the beach? A beach with no ocean? Endless beach, and no ocean? Kill me.

PATRICK. I mean, they have the sea there, they have –

MARCELLE. I know that. It was a – forget it.

PATRICK. So you're not going.

MARCELLE. I don't know.

PATRICK. What does that mean?

MARCELLE. It means, I Do Not Know, what I am doing. I'm not single. I don't get to make this decision on my own. I'm part of a family, I'm part of a couple, there's a lot to weigh.

PATRICK. There's nothing to weigh. Your son is going through a phase, he's – how long has he been doing this whole Jewish thing?

MARCELLE. This Jewish thing?

PATRICK. You know what I – it's a phase. You don't move to a new country for a phase. Look at me! I walk down the street every day, I'm fine. I'm absolutely fine –

MARCELLE. It's not about feeling scared for Daniel, per se, but...

PATRICK. But what?

MARCELLE. Charles feels – and I don't disagree, necessarily –

PATRICK. Necessarily –

MARCELLE. The fact that, when we expose ourselves, in public, as Jews, we double triple quadruple the chances of violent attacks – that *that* exposes something about how people really feel. And the only way our people have stayed alive all these years is either –

PATRICK. Our people –

MARCELLE. Is either we –

PATRICK. You sound like you're in a cult. *Our* people –

MARCELLE. Is either we have been lucky, or we got out before it was too late. And he would know. He watched his family make that decision when he was a kid. He knows the signs.

PATRICK. What signs? Are there incidents? Yes, there are incidents. Guess what? It's not safe anywhere, not anywhere, no matter who you are. In America they shoot people at the movies, at night clubs, they don't care. How many people were killed in Nice last summer? People of all stripes? More people died in Nice than all these Jewish attacks combined. So let's say you never went to synagogue, you never did anything quote unquote Jewish, but one day you go to celebrate Bastille day and all of a sudden –

MARCELLE. I would never have been there –

PATRICK. You don't know.

MARCELLE. I would not have been there –

PATRICK. You don't know –

MARCELLE. I don't go to the beach Patrick, I know. I wouldn't be caught dead, in July, outside, in a crowd of people, to watch fireworks! That is not something I would do that is actually one of my recurring nightmares, so no.

PATRICK. You know what I'm saying. It's all, it's indiscriminate.

MARCELLE. It's actually not.

PATRICK. It's mostly indiscriminate.

MARCELLE. Mostly mostly mostly. That's the key word.

PATRICK. Look, just – use your brain here, OK?

MARCELLE. I'm trying to use my brain, Patrick. That is what I am trying to do. And part of my brain tells me, when I went to visit Israel I thought it was a perfectly interesting country, and I couldn't wait to get home. Part of my brain tells me I am as French as anyone, and no one and nothing is going to push me out of my own country. When you feel like you're under attack, when your country is quite seriously considering electing a woman from the National Front, the *National Front*, the party that refers to Nazi gas chambers as a quote unquote "point of detail," when you find yourself in that situation you stay and you fight, because you have a right to live in your country as much as anyone, *anyone*, and while there may be a few bad people, that's not a reason to leave because guess what there are bad people everywhere. But. Part of my brain also reminds me, we grew up without a grandmother, without aunts, with almost no cousins to speak of and why? Because they didn't leave when they could. So I better be damn sure, when the man I trust the most in this world tells me he's scared, that I think long and hard about what he sees that maybe I don't, or you don't, and pay attention.

PATRICK. And what does Papa think of your big plans?

MARCELLE. There are no plans, there's no reason for him to know any of this so just, shah.

PATRICK. Cause if you think you can just leave him for me
to take care of –

MARCELLE. Oh, oh, the way you've left me to do all the
taking care of him for the last, oh, ten years –

PATRICK. That's not true!

MARCELLE. It's *mostly* true.

<table>
<tr><td>PATRICK.</td><td>MARCELLE.</td></tr>
<tr><td>I'm the one who's always
saying, it's time to give
up that store.</td><td>Mostly, mostly, mostly…</td></tr>
</table>

MARCELLE. Well that's not happening.

PATRICK. He's fallen down there twice, so… twice.

MARCELLE. Yeah and who brought him to the hospital?
Both times?

PATRICK. I'm just saying –

MARCELLE. And I'm just saying – don't tell me he's fallen
twice when I'm the one who dealt with it – twice! That
piano store is maybe the only thing left that brings him
any joy. Who are we to take that from him?

PATRICK. It's not safe.

MARCELLE. He's eighty-six Patrick, if his dream is to lose
his balance and crack his skull on the back of a piano,
who are we to stop him?

PATRICK. I'd really like if we could be on the same page
about this.

MARCELLE. Well we're not. OK? I'm not on the same page
as anyone. I live on my own page. I live in my own
book. And if one more person asks me to get on the
same page I'm going to put six rocks in my pocket, take
myself down to the Seine and just fucking fling myself
into it, OK?

PATRICK. So you're what, you're just packed? Ready to go at a moment's notice?

MARCELLE. What?

PATRICK. What's with the suitcase?

MARCELLE. Oh. Oh. Ugh. Molly.

PATRICK. She's still here?

MARCELLE. Every weekend. I said she could come one fucking weekend, now I can't get rid of her.

PATRICK. It's your house.

MARCELLE. I'm not the one inviting her.

Daniel claims they're just friends, they just enjoy hanging out.

PATRICK. Uh huh. Hanging out, every weekend?

MARCELLE. Every weekend for two months.

PATRICK. Good friends, huh?

MARCELLE. First she was homesick. Then she was, I don't know. Then Clinton lost, she was in mourning.

PATRICK. She should be.

MARCELLE. I've never seen someone cry so hard. "I can't believe my country would do this, I can't *believe* my country would do this." It's sweet, actually. You forget when you're young, the world can still break your heart.

PATRICK. So where is this little kissing cousin?

(Quick beat.)

MARCELLE. I made Elodie take her out.

*(**MARCELLE** laughs.)*

PATRICK. Good luck Molly.

MARCELLE. Good luck indeed.

*(They laugh, **PATRICK** smiles.)*

PATRICK. Things are fine, everything's going to be fine. You guys, you – you always see the glass half empty. It's a sour way to live.

MARCELLE. Thank you so much for pointing that out, that's really helpful.

PATRICK. Who was it? Anne Frank – it was – Anne Frank who said, after everything, I still believe people are good. After *everything*. That's what Anne Frank said. Think about that.

MARCELLE. Yes, she did say that, and a few months later she was dead, so. Think about *that*.

(Lights shift.)

*(**ELODIE** and **MOLLY**, out at a bar. **ELODIE** has probably said "this is my last point" eight or nine times before this moment.)*

ELODIE. No this is my last, last, final point.

*(**ELODIE** takes a huge swig of whatever she's been drinking, then goes on.)*

To be a Jew in Europe, to be a Jew in France, is to grow up in a place that has historically, for hundreds and in some cases thousands of years, persecuted you, in every generation, and when I say persecute I don't mean they wouldn't let you into the nice country club I mean rape. I mean death. I mean, stealing everything that is yours and then making you pay taxes on the things *they* stole. American Jews don't know what that feels like, not personally. And don't get me wrong, I'm not suggesting there isn't a raging antisemitism in your country, of course there is, and who's to say what gets unleashed by your new "president," maybe the whole thing's about to change, in which case, you know, welcome to the club but my point is, when your ancestors left Europe,

America was the Holy land, the promised land, and while the history of antisemitism in America could fill perhaps a chapter or two of a book, it is not *the* book. That's not to say America is blameless – the opposite is true, obviously. And of course France is not innocent either – you're living in Nantes, you've I assume been to the memorial they now have dedicated to their role in the slave trade, the city's financial wealth was all built on the back of that, and no one talked about it – but name a country that hasn't tortured segments of its population – you can't. And while the American Jew descends from the refugee who fled persecution, he himself is not a victim of persecution, and so he is the first Jew in history who – how do I explain this?

So when my grandmother died, my father's mother – she was Algerian, then she fled to France she was French – when she died, I had this weird feeling she felt – not that she was *relieved* but that, the rules of history are such that she was supposed to die at the hands of someone else, in some hideous and horrible way, but instead, she got to die in her bed, propped up on a pillow, surrounded by her family, and while most people assume that's a normal way to go, for a Jew, if you get to die in a deathbed, even though you're dying you weirdly feel lucky – and obviously I'm surmising, since I haven't died myself, but I saw it with my grandmother. American Jews don't experience that, they feel pretty free. So when it comes to Israel, they either despise it, or they're slavishly devoted to it because they have a deep-seated understanding in their bones, that there has never been a country on Earth that hasn't eventually at some point turned on its Jews, and even in America, that fate awaits them too. I mean, look at the Jews of Spain – look at Ladino – you know what Ladino is?

*(Before **MOLLY** can say "no," **ELODIE** continues.)*

Ladino was the language of Spanish Jews, a mix of Spanish and Hebrew – like Yiddish, but with Spanish instead of German – today there are very few speakers left, almost none, but my point is, it is actually *breathtaking* to imagine a moment in time when Jews felt so secure, they invented a whole new language perfectly suited to that country. I mean, you don't invent a *language,* unless you feel *really* fucking at home somewhere, and of course we know how that turned out – expelled, forced conversions, burned at the stake, the works – American Jews haven't done that, there's no combination of Hebrew and, I don't even know, Valley Girl? – which suggests they understand that America, which has been their home and given them refuge may turn on them someday, perhaps sooner than they realize, I mean, stay tuned, right? So. Then you have the American Jew who hates Israel or is highly critical of Israel and I would argue part of why they feel able to be so critical of Israel is because they feel so safe in America, because they've convinced themselves that they can stay in America forever and maybe that's true now but if history is our guide and history must always be our guide then you have to ask, so you feel safe today but will that be the case a hundred years from now? Or ten?

MOLLY. I just think –

ELODIE. Hold on, let me just finish this – I don't have an issue with criticism of the state of Israel, I know some see that as a betrayal, or an act of self-hatred but I think it's honorable, or it can be – sometimes it's performative, like look at me I'm not one of *those* disgusting Jews I'm a different kind of Jew I'm a genius enlightened Jew who shits on Israel love me hug me kiss me fuck me, *that,* I fucking hate – but the Jew who holds Israel to the highest standards because they believe we have an obligation to always strive to be more just and righteous and honorable, *that* I applaud, *that* I think, yes, yes, I want *that.*

MOLLY. I'm sorry, but I'm only following about half of what you're saying –

ELODIE. The problem is, we are a tiny minority, we cannot survive without allies, so then the question becomes, where do we turn? You can get in bed with the right, but they're also in bed with the *far*-right, and let's be real, *far-right* is just a polite way of saying Nazi, and I don't know about you, but I don't get in bed with Nazis, and I'm not about to accept the occasional bone they'll throw me so they can take cover behind me and pretend they're decent and then go off and commit whatever atrocities they're gonna commit to appease that far-right base which we already established is just another word for NAZIS. Not happening! So you think, OK – let's get as far from the far-right as possible so you run to the left but that's a whole other shitshow because every lefty will tell you their opinion of Benjamin Netanyahu but I guarantee, you ask what they think of the Prime Minister of India, half of them couldn't even tell you that man's name and what's worse is they don't stop to interrogate why. Why do they know so much more about Israel than almost anywhere else in the world because combined, Israel and Palestine *combined* have about thirteen million people. Do you know what the population of India is? Do you? One point three BILLION people. We're talking a HUNDRED times more people. Do you see a HUNDRED times more news stories about India than Israel? Do you? And they say *we* control the media? Indonesia has TWENTY times as many people. Twenty times. Forget getting twenty times as many articles, when do you hear ANYTHING about what goes on in Indonesia? Nigeria, Pakistan, Bangladesh all have more than a HUNDRED MILLION citizens. You think your average person in France has an opinion on the state of Bangladesh? But I guarantee you they have an opinion on Israel, maybe if we heard about what was going on in Indonesia even half as often as we read about

Israel our collective priorities would shift a little but everyone is just obsessed with Israel and you have to ask why? This is the question. Why? Why when there's so many awful things in the world, this becomes your obsession. Why? You have to interrogate it Molly you have to, this is a *must*. Why do so many rallies against Israel devolve into rallies where people are screaming Death to Israel and then Death to Jews. Death? This is what they scream, on the streets of Paris, in my own ears I have heard it ring out, death to Jews, why is that? Anytime things flare up between Israel and Palestine – Jews – in other countries – get attacked. If hating Israel has nothing to do with hating Jews, why does that happen? Every time? Like clockwork? Or is everyone just ahistorical?

Because – and don't get me wrong: I don't think Israel is perfect, but tell me, what country is?

MOLLY. Are you familiar with this thing called whataboutism?

ELODIE. I mean, America gets attacked one time – once – and they're off to war in the Middle East, for years –

MOLLY. Wait, are – are we on 9/11 now?

ELODIE. And don't misunderstand me, I am not minimizing 9/11, I would never minimize – never –

MOLLY. Oh my god, we're on 9/11 –

ELODIE. That was an atrocity, I believe that to my core – that said, America is attacked one time once, and suddenly they're sending troops into Iraq for reasons we still don't understand – gas? oil? – alongside the British, who then have the *gall* to condemn other countries? Are you KIDDING me? I mean, oh my god Molly, don't get me started on the British, please don't get me started on the British.

MOLLY. I'd actually love it if we could skip the British –

ELODIE. What country, on this planet has brought more suffering and destruction everywhere it has gone –

MOLLY. But – but most people I know think the war in Iraq was wrong.

ELODIE. You can *think* whatever you like, but your tax dollars paid for that war, you see what I'm saying?

MOLLY. Uh, no, I don't –

ELODIE. A belief – what is a belief – you *think*, who cares what you *think*. You love the war, you hate the war – either way, your *actions* are the same. You paid taxes. Your parents paid taxes. Your dollars speak louder than any words, and your dollars support the war.

MOLLY. Well by that logic –

ELODIE. Let me finish –

MOLLY. No by that logic – by your own logic, if dollars speak louder than words, and my country gives *billions* of dollars to Israel, and I don't like how *my* money is being spent, don't I have a responsibility – an obligation – to speak up? Sure I could protest human rights violations in Myanmar or Iran or wherever, but my government's not sending billions of dollars to those countries, so my protest might be justified but I'd just be shouting into the wind –

ELODIE. Then shout about Egypt! They get billions from America, too – they share a border with Gaza, too – where are the protests about Egypt? What do you think Egypt is doing with your billions? Putting up solar panels?

MOLLY. We could go back and forth like this all night, but...

ELODIE. And that's my point! That's exactly my point!

MOLLY. What is?

ELODIE. History *demands* we go back and forth all night, you can't understand one thing without understanding everything, but who takes the time to do that anymore? And so everyone has become completely ahistorical! They have no memory, and *that* is my point, because what happened to us is documented, it's all documented, there's a reason they call us the people of the book, if you want to know what happened to the people of the book then READ THE FUCKING BOOK, we didn't *go* on a cruise for two thousand years you fucking idiots but that's my point, that is my fucking point because who reads books anymore no one reads no one even knows what history is, and that is the real problem, the real real problem is that most people? Are just stupid. Most people are so stupid it actually breaks my heart, so what you end up with are these debates raging online between people who are stupid to begin with and then basically massively uninformed but because of the internet, they fancy themselves experts in everything when the only thing they have expertise in is how to waste a perfectly good life, but they watch one YouTube video which reduces three thousand years of complex, dense, complicated history into a two minute summary of events and they're suddenly screaming about something they know nothing about and what's worse is this doesn't just pass for debate in a hundred and forty characters, this becomes policy! This is how policy gets made and it's so fucking depressing it makes me want to blow my brains out. And this is my point.

MOLLY. *This* is your point?

ELODIE. This is my point, I just need to make this one point and this is my point, my point is my brother is kind and he's good and he's sweet, and I know that. And I can see that you see that too, so –

MOLLY. Wait, what –

ELODIE. My brother. He's a good person.

MOLLY. OK. Uhm. Why are you telling me this?

ELODIE. Because he likes you.

MOLLY. What? No, we're – we're just friends.

ELODIE. You like him, and my brother, he likes you.

MOLLY. How do you, I mean, has he told you, he –

ELODIE. And my brother, when he likes someone, he can become… susceptible, he can be very easily influenced by them.

MOLLY. In what way?

ELODIE. Look what he wears on his head!

MOLLY. You mean, his kippah?

ELODIE. You think he woke up one morning and found God?

MOLLY. He said it was, it was snowing in Paris one night and –

ELODIE. Oh my god that fucking story – the snow – no – he met a girl, he met a girl who was religious, he started to go round with her, and then…

MOLLY. Then what?

ELODIE. She dropped him but this is my point. Two years later, and he's still, kippah à la rosh, so, all I'm saying is, I know you think you know my brother, you've spent time with him, you've seen him playing guitar without his shirt which, I get it, Mohammed has told me enough times how cute he is, my friends are all obsessed – you're here for a few months, then you fly back to America and get to live your life however you want, supporting Israel, protesting Israel, either way it costs you nothing. For you, it's a purely intellectual exercise. For us, we don't get the luxury of having an opinion about Israel, or that piece of shit Netanyahu – because we might need Israel. And soon. And when you need something, when you're out of options, you forfeit your right to an opinion. So please: Don't make this harder for my family than it already is.

>   *(Beat.)*

MOLLY. You just spent the last hour railing against people who are uninformed. Now you're asking me to stay silent so your brother can remain uninformed about perspectives he's not getting from anywhere else.

ELODIE. No I just think –

MOLLY. No no no I just think, if you're a person who values an informed debate, you can't be scared of information.

ELODIE. I'm not.

MOLLY. Good. Then you have nothing to fear from me. I'm no expert, I never said I was. But I do read, and I am learning, and I am trying to be a little less like those idiots you find so – what'd you call them? Ahistorical. But, like you said, information doesn't scare you, so. I couldn't possibly be a threat to you, or your family.

ELODIE. I never said threat.

MOLLY. You didn't have to.

The reality is, your brother and I don't talk about Israel.

But. If we do, you can be sure I will not hesitate to let him know *exactly* what I think.

>   *(A very long beat.* **ELODIE** *takes out a cigarette, lights it, begins to smoke.)*

ELODIE. You have a very strong point of view.

I like this.

MOLLY. I don't know that my point of view is so strong. I – the America I left, four months ago, feels like a different universe. It was always flawed, we knew that, but we had – even if we didn't always live up to our ideals, at least we had ideals to fall short of – and to strive towards, but it's like everyone just… forgot. And everything's about to change. And everyone I know is… petrified. So when you say it's all theoretical for me? You have no idea how scared I am.

(**ELODIE** *reaches for* **MOLLY**'s *hand.*)

ELODIE. Of course you're scared. The world is on fire.

(Lights shift.)

(**YOUNG PIERRE** *approaches a framed photograph, picks it up, and stares at it for a beat. He is alone in this room, for the first time since his return, free of the watchful eyes of adults.)*

(He listens as his father and grandparents talk offstage, down the hall.)

LUCIEN. *(Offstage.)* I'm not – no – I'm not doing anything until I check on the store –

IRMA. *(Offstage.)* The store is fine. That boy needs to see a doctor first.

ADOLPHE. *(Offstage.)* I told him, the inventory was sold, but –

LUCIEN. *(Offstage.)* First we are going to check on the store.

IRMA. *(Offstage.)* The store is fine.

ADOLPHE. *(Offstage.)* The inventory was sold, but the store is fine.

LUCIEN. *(Offstage.)* But there were, what – three fifty? Four hundred? I couldn't give those pianos away.

ADOLPHE. *(Offstage.)* Then things came back around. They always do. It's all circles.

IRMA. *(Offstage.)* I am worried about him, Lucien, I am.

LUCIEN. *(Offstage.)* But – who bought them?

ADOLPHE. *(Offstage.)* You'd have to ask Irene.

LUCIEN. *(Offstage.)* Who buys four hundred pianos in the middle of a war?

IRMA. *(Offstage.)* A doctor needs to see Pierre – a good one. Who knows what he has –

ADOLPHE. *(Offstage.)* Circles.

IRMA. *(Offstage.)* Or what happened where you were, or – Who knows!

ADOLPHE. *(Offstage.)* It's all circles.

LUCIEN. *(Offstage.)* Thank you yes, it's so helpful when you repeat yourself, please tell me more about circles.

IRMA. *(Offstage.)* You upset your father.

ADOLPHE. *(Offstage.)* I'm not upset.

IRMA. *(Offstage.)* Of course you are.

LUCIEN. *(Offstage.)* I'm sorry, it's just...

ADOLPHE. *(Offstage.)* It'll come back around.

LUCIEN. *(Offstage.)* I know, I just, I thought I'd have something to sell...

(**PIERRE** *puts down the photo and exits.*)

(*Lights shift.*)

(**MARCELLE** *sits with her laptop, working.*)

(*Offstage, the front door opens.* **CHARLES** *enters, wheeling on a suitcase.* **MARCELLE** *doesn't turn around, and says nothing.*)

(**CHARLES** *senses she is ignoring him, but waits to be acknowledged.* **MARCELLE** *keeps working. So he sits down beside her.*)

MARCELLE. I'm working.

CHARLES. I see that.

MARCELLE. Where's Daniel?

CHARLES. He went to meet friends.

MARCELLE. *(You mean Molly.)* Friends?

CHARLES. You didn't respond to my texts.

MARCELLE. I'm working.

CHARLES. All weekend, you didn't respond.

MARCELLE. I was working all weekend.

CHARLES. I would never do anything you didn't want, too.

MARCELLE. You're a grown man do whatever you like.

CHARLES. I'd like to be with you. Wherever you are, that's
for me.

*(A long beat. **MARCELLE** stops, takes him in.)*

MARCELLE. I thought you were scared.

CHARLES. I am.

MARCELLE. So?

CHARLES. So, I'll be scared here.

MARCELLE. But if you're scared, I mean, you think
something could happen?

CHARLES. Yes.

MARCELLE. Like what?

CHARLES. I don't know. What's the worst that happens?
I die? So I die.

MARCELLE. What if someone hurts Daniel?

CHARLES. Then he would die.

MARCELLE. Don't say that!

CHARLES. What should I say?

MARCELLE. I couldn't go on.

CHARLES. You'd go on.

MARCELLE. I couldn't.

CHARLES. You'd go on, Marcelle. You come from a long line of people who had to bury their children and found a way to go on. Probably more Jewish parents have had to bury a child than not. That's how it is.

MARCELLE. I don't want to bury a child.

CHARLES. And hopefully we never will.

(Beat.)

MARCELLE. Did you like it?

CHARLES. Yes.

MARCELLE. Did you see apartments?

CHARLES. Yes.

MARCELLE. Were they nice?

CHARLES. You wouldn't think so, but –

MARCELLE. Why wouldn't I think so?

CHARLES. Marcelle. Do I know you at all? You would have *haaaaaaated* these apartments.

MARCELLE. So they weren't nice?

CHARLES. No. They were very nice.

MARCELLE. Then why would I hate them?

CHARLES. Because I know you!

MARCELLE. I don't hate very nice things.

CHARLES. OK.

(Quick beat.)

MARCELLE. A lot of people come back. They go, they can't make it work, or they can't find work, they can't adjust. Two, three years later, they come back to France.

CHARLES. Did you get my ingredients, to make my –

MARCELLE. Did you hear me? I said a lot of people come back –

CHARLES. I heard you.

MARCELLE. And?

CHARLES. You don't have to convince me anymore. You're here, I want to be with you, that's it. I accept our fate, whatever it is.

MARCELLE. That's dark.

CHARLES. What do you want me to say? I'm staying with you. OK?

MARCELLE. And – Daniel?

CHARLES. He was happy, Marcelle, he was… He walked down the street, no one stared, no one bothered him. It was… good. He wants to finish the school year first – fine. He promised to wear his cap when he goes out – great. So. Let me make my donuts for Channukah. Did you get my ingredients?

> (**MARCELLE** *nods. Lights shift.*)

> (**LUCIEN** *and* **ADOLPHE** *enter and go to the table.*)

LUCIEN. I just thought – I thought I'd have something to sell.

ADOLPHE. What can I tell you? Irene managed to unload the pianos.

LUCIEN. No, good, but – how?

ADOLPHE. Soldiers.

LUCIEN. Soldiers?

ADOLPHE. On their way out, they bought them cheap, shipped them home to Germany.

LUCIEN. German soldiers bought our pianos?

ADOLPHE. Souvenirs from Paris. Somewhere, a Nazi's daughter is playing Bach on a Salomon.

LUCIEN. Well. Enjoy.

(*Quick beat.*)

ADOLPHE. A couple months, you'll see, factories will be up and running, you'll have new pianos to sell.

LUCIEN. A couple months?

ADOLPHE. A couple months. Five, six months.

LUCIEN. Dad, a couple is two. *Two* is a couple.

ADOLPHE. So a few months. Six months.

(**PIERRE** *enters, carrying shoes.*)

LUCIEN. Think pal: June July August September October – *November.* You know what that means? New pianos to sell a month before...

PIERRE. Christmas.

ADOLPHE. Ehhhhy.

(**ADOLPHE** *opens his arms a bit, as if to say, could you ask for better timing?*)

LUCIEN. Cause there's gonna be a lot of demand, a lot. Cause people need music. Especially after... they need pianos. Right?

(*To himself.*) Who the fuck buys a piano right after a war?

(**IRMA** *joins them.* **PATRICK** *emerges.* **PIERRE** *ties his shoes.*)

PATRICK. Picture them, that first morning back, getting ready to check on the store. What did they talk about? Did Irma stare at her son, burning a hole through him, desperate to know...

IRMA. Tell me.

PATRICK. Did he ignore her? Or say:

LUCIEN. Not now. Not ever.

IRMA. Not ever?

PATRICK. Or deflect, turn to Pierre and say:

LUCIEN. Your shoelace is untied.

YOUNG PIERRE. I know...

LUCIEN. Just...

IRMA. Not ever?

ADOLPHE. Irma – stop.

IRMA. I'm not talking to you, I'm talking to Lucien.

ADOLPHE. Well talk to me, OK?

IRMA. I'm sick of talking to you.

ADOLPHE. That's the spirit.

(*Quick beat.*)

YOUNG PIERRE. When did you get back?

IRMA. Get back?

YOUNG PIERRE. To Paris?

ADOLPHE. We stayed.

IRMA. We didn't leave.

YOUNG PIERRE. But what happened when they arrested you?

ADOLPHE. They didn't.

IRMA. We were lucky.

YOUNG PIERRE. Oh.

> *(Beat.)*

PATRICK. And when they got to the store, what did they think as they rounded the corner, and looked up?

> *(They turn from their places in the apartment, suddenly on the street. All but* **ADOLPHE** *look up at the store.)*

Painted across the side of the building, right there in the street, for anyone to see:

Pianos… Salomon. Like some cave drawing, from a way of life long gone.

My grandfather Lucien lived until I was seven. When I think of him, he's at the store, surrounded by pianos to sell. But how he managed that?

> *(***PATRICK*** shrugs.)*

They'll put up a plaque for victims. But the people who find a way forward, with children to feed and nothing to their name but their name itself? There's no plaque for that.

> *(As the* **SALOMONS** *leave with* **PATRICK,** **MOLLY** *emerges with* **DANIEL,** *who puts on a baseball cap.)*

DANIEL. Don't listen to my sister. *Elodie* doesn't even believe half the stuff she says. She just likes to argue.

MOLLY. I could tell.

DANIEL. Because, I'm my own person. I'm not, what'd she call me?

MOLLY. I don't want to –

DANIEL. No, just, what'd she call me?

MOLLY. Susceptible.

DANIEL. Yeah. That's not true. I'm, like, the least susceptible person I know, so. You can share any views you want.

MOLLY. Uhm, I'm good, thanks.

DANIEL. But I like hearing different points of view.

MOLLY. Well lucky for you, someone invented the internet!

DANIEL. I should never have let my sister near you.

MOLLY. I actually kind of liked talking to her.

DANIEL. Please.

MOLLY. I did. It was informative.

DANIEL. About...

MOLLY. You. Mostly.

DANIEL. Oh god. What'd she tell you? Oh god.

ELODIE. You play guitar?

DANIEL. Not, like, super well, but...

MOLLY. Without your shirt on?

DANIEL. Oh. Oh, that's – humiliating.

MOLLY. I've never seen you do that.

DANIEL. That's... only if I'm around the house or, if no one's around or whatever.

MOLLY. What do you play?

DANIEL. I don't know. My Dad's uhm, obsessed with American music. We were basically raised on Bob Dylan.

MOLLY. I like Bob Dylan.

DANIEL. *(Smiling.)* You want me to take my shirt off and play some Bob Dylan?

(**MOLLY** *smiles.*)

Everyone's asleep.

MOLLY. You could whisper.

(**MOLLY** *and* **DANIEL** *return to the apartment, but when they get there, they find* **CHARLES**, *awake, preparing donuts, maybe rocking out a little to some Bob Dylan.**)

DANIEL. Oh. You're still up.

CHARLES. I'm still up.

(**CHARLES** *turns down the volume.*)

You two want to help, I'll finish sooner, the sooner I finish, the sooner I go to bed...

(**DANIEL** *looks at* **MOLLY**, *taking his cue from her.*)

MOLLY. Definitely.

CHARLES. Great. All I'm doing is rolling them out, flour your hands, and grab some dough – not too much.

MOLLY. OK.

CHARLES. (*As they roll.*) It's not hard, they'll puff up overnight. Then tomorrow we fry them in oil, of course – oil everything, the miracle of Channukah – you don't have to overwork it – squirt a little jelly inside, some powdered sugar, and we're set.

You're a natural.

MOLLY. It's relaxing, actually.

CHARLES. It is, isn't it?

MOLLY. This is a family recipe?

DANIEL. Yeah, it was my grandma's, and probably her grandma's before her.

---

* A license to produce *PRAYER FOR THE FRENCH REPUBLIC* does not include a performance license for any third-party or copyrighted recordings. Licensees should create their own.

MOLLY. Oh wow, really?

CHARLES. No.

DANIEL. Yes it is.

CHARLES. The recipe comes from... an ex-girlfriend. Before Marcelle.

DANIEL. Wait, what?

CHARLES. My family thinks it's straight out of grandma's kitchen, but... no.

DANIEL. Does Mom know?

CHARLES. No and there's no reason she needs to, so. Shhh...

DANIEL. Oh my god! You just destroyed my childhood!

CHARLES. You'll be OK.

DANIEL. Oh my god!

CHARLES. Come, roll. Let's make grandma's donuts.

DANIEL. Not funny.

> (**CHARLES** *purposely bumps into* **DANIEL,** *nudging him.)*

MOLLY. Your mother was from Algeria?

CHARLES. And me. My whole family, everyone. Going back five hundred years.

MOLLY. Wow.

CHARLES. And Spain before that. Probably fourteen hundred years in Spain, before the Inquisition.

MOLLY. What was it like, in Algeria?

CHARLES. I was just a kid when we left.

MOLLY. Yeah.

CHARLES. But I remember the kitchen. The smell… that's the most powerful sense. It was an Arabic kitchen, you know, couscous and spices. We felt Arab – we were. In Algeria, we all lived together, everyone got along, it was, you know, all the kids growing up together, you'd maybe, you'd go have a snack at this one's house, they'd come have a snack at your house. It was a nice way to grow up. But…

MOLLY. You felt, you had to leave?

CHARLES. Oh, there was no choice, absolutely no choice. And then we came here but, no one knew what to make of us, the French Jews didn't. I had much more in common with Muslims in Algeria. The Jews in France, they were still in shock from World War II, trying to fade into the background. Then we showed up, talking loud, laughing loud. We hadn't gone through what they had. I've heard them say it was like we came and started dancing in the streets. No shame, no fear. We felt free. And we were, for a time. It was beautiful.

(Quick beat.)

MOLLY. I imagine, if you have to leave your home, that's something you only want to do once. I can't imagine, doing that twice, in one lifetime…

CHARLES. Well. Imagine.

DANIEL. If Grandma were alive, she'd be *chaining* herself to the Bastille. Iron chains. You'd have to drag her from here, kicking and screaming. She loved France.

CHARLES. And she had loved Algeria. But she left. Then she came here, she loved it here. You can learn to love it anywhere.

DANIEL. You think so?

CHARLES. I know so.

This is what the Benhamous do. We just keep criss-crossing the Mediterranean, just back and forth and back and forth until forever. Spain, Algeria, France…

Always on the go, always moving, never…

> *(He drops his hands, to suggest putting something down, settled.)*

Always wandering…

But what can you do? It's the suitcase, or the coffin.

> *(Lights shift.)*

> *(**IRMA**, **ADOLPHE**, and **LUCIEN** are sitting down to play cards. **LUCIEN** is dealing.)*

IRMA. Lucien.

LUCIEN. I'm trying to count.

IRMA. We're really going to sit around playing cards, like nothing happened?

LUCIEN. Yep. Now do you want to start, or shall I?

IRMA. What I want, is to talk about what happened.

ADOLPHE. Irma.

IRMA. Almost two years without a word from you, I want to know.

ADOLPHE. Stop.

LUCIEN. I'm here now, that's enough.

IRMA. You're my son. I need to know.

ADOLPHE. Stop!

LUCIEN. Trust me: You don't want to know.

IRMA. Trust me: I do.

ADOLPHE. For godssake, Irma, stop.

IRMA. Stop telling me to stop! You've been telling me to stop all day, *you* stop! You of all people. You were with me, here in this apartment, meal after meal, at this table, *this* table, for two years, while I was losing my mind, never knowing where the children were, how they were, what was happening – not knowing anything! Not knowing, my mind running away with the most frightening, the most – so much worse, letting your mind imagine – so much worse than knowing the truth not knowing not knowing never knowing –

LUCIEN. What do you want to know, Mom? What? We went to Poland! They split us up! What do you want to know?

IRMA. I want to know!

LUCIEN. You want to know how I watched them rip Colette's little purse out of her hands and throw it onto a pile of other people's shit? How I helped my father-in-law into a truck and never saw him again? What exactly do you want to know, huh? What? What? WHAT?

IRMA. I want to know what happened to the girls!

LUCIEN. They're dead! OK! They're dead! They're fucking dead! I love you! OK? I love you. I –

(*Before* **LUCIEN** *can go on,* **YOUNG PIERRE** *enters.*)

(*All eyes are on him. He moves past the grown-ups to the piano, sits, and begins to play. It is lovely and simple, and stops his father from having to go on.*)

(*On the other side of the stage, without our being able to hear,* **MARCELLE'S FAMILY** *lights the candles for the first night of Channukah.*)

(**PATRICK** *emerges, to watch.*)

(**YOUNG PIERRE** *plays a little more. This young boy, surrounded on one side by the people who raised him, and on the other side of the stage, his future descendents, people he cannot begin to imagine. But they are all there, five generations of Salomons in Paris, listening to this young survivor of Auschwitz play piano.*)

(*The music grows louder, and then:*)

(*Blackout.*)

ACT THREE

(Lights up on the **BENHAMOUS**, *in their dining room.)*

(Seder, 2017.)

*(***CHARLES** *stands at the head of the table.)*

CHARLES. This is the bread of affliction,
the poor bread,
which our ancestors ate in the land of Egypt.
Let all who are hungry come and eat.
Let all who are in want share the hope of Passover.
As we celebrate here, we join with our people everywhere.
This year we celebrate here.
Next year in... the land of Israel.
Now we are still in bonds.
Next year may all be free.

*(***CHARLES** *sits, as* **PATRICK** *enters.)*

PATRICK. After a mild winter, in the early days of spring, 2017, the Benhamous gathered for Passover. Marcelle and I were not raised with this holiday. But I would sometimes come, and silently marvel at how my sister had mastered this ancient ritual, which had surely been celebrated for generations in our family – until it wasn't, until Marcelle rescued it from the lost and found.

I watched my nephew and niece lead us through the ceremony, as my own daughters never could.

DANIEL. Karpas. Greens for spring, dipped in salt water, a symbol of the tears shed by our ancestors.

ELODIE. Maror. Bitter herbs. The harshness of slavery, reduced to a single bite of horseradish.

PATRICK. And at this seder, I was not the only guest.

CHARLES. And this is Molly.

PATRICK. Ohhhh.

MOLLY. In every generation, each of us should feel as though we ourselves had gone forth from Egypt.

ELODIE. *(Handing maror to* **MOLLY.***)* Bitter herbs?

DANIEL. In every generation, in every age, some rise up to plot our annihilation. But a divine power sustains and delivers us.

PATRICK. After the Seder, we had our meal, which was one-quarter eating, three-quarters arguing.

ELODIE. This is my last, last, final point.

PATRICK. No! No more points Elodie. She'll never win, so...

ELODIE. But that's not the point! She's going to make the top two, and *that's* what's so upsetting, and *that's* my point –

PATRICK. But France will never elect Le Pen.

ELODIE. Oh my god, Uncle Patrick, you're smarter than that. Is it actually inconceivable to you that a democratic nation could elect a monster? Please.

CHARLES. *(To* **MOLLY.***)* We have an election in two weeks, for President.

MOLLY. Yes, I've been following. And you – you do it in two parts?

CHARLES. Yes, round one has lots of candidates to choose from, then the top two face off two weeks later.

DANIEL. For a while it looked like Fillon's to lose, but...

ELODIE. That was before the nepotism scandal, so it'll probably be Macron who's neither right nor left, but –

PATRICK. But he will defeat her in the end.

CHARLES. You actually don't know that.

DANIEL. Le Pen's party is the National Front, they're kind of like...

ELODIE. Nazis. They're Nazis.

DANIEL. They're not Nazis, but, historically, they've been sympathizers.

ELODIE. With Nazis.

DANIEL. And they're xenophobic, and Islamophobic.

ELODIE. It's a charming party, she leads.

PATRICK. I kept waiting for my sister to jump in, she usually dominated family conversation, but she was quiet that night. Unusually so.

MARCELLE. *(To everyone.)* All done?

(**MARCELLE** *begins to clear. Beat.*)

PATRICK. When do you return to America?

MOLLY. At the end of the month.

PATRICK. And have you enjoyed yourself in France?

MOLLY. Enjoy doesn't – putting all else aside – just the croissants – the croissants alone – on your block – on your *block*.

CHARLES. They're not bad, right?

PATRICK. And you've done all the things, seen all the sites?

MOLLY. Just about. Except, you know, the best free concert in Paris, apparently.

PATRICK. What concert is that?

MOLLY. I was told someone at this table gives the best Bob Dylan serenade –

DANIEL. *(To* **ELODIE**.*)* Thanks a lot.

ELODIE. It was in the context of a much larger discussion about the Israeli–Palestinian conflict.

PATRICK. Huh?

ELODIE. I can go into it, if you want –

DANIEL.

Don't!

PATRICK.

No!

CHARLES. Daniel does have a beautiful voice. We find him out here, playing guitar, no shirt – pants, but no shirt –

DANIEL. Oh my god!

ELODIE. He's very into the shirtless kippah look.

DANIEL. And, we're done.

MOLLY. Well I'd love to see it sometime.

ELODIE. Awww. Cousins.

PATRICK. As Marcelle continued clearing, the kids were sent to look for the afikomen, though Elodie refused.

*(**DANIEL** and **MOLLY** rise to look.)*

ELODIE. The whole notion of the afikomen is antisemitic.

CHARLES. It's part of our tradition. Our own tradition can't be antisemitic!

ELODIE. Fine, let me rephrase: this section perpetuates a lot of antisemitic tropes I don't think are helpful.

CHARLES. But you haven't even looked for it. You haven't even –

DANIEL. Too late.

*(**DANIEL** holds up the afikomen.)*

CHARLES. Already?

DANIEL. You stick it in the same place every year.

CHARLES. Yes but this is reverse psychology – Marcelle –
isn't this reverse psychology?

MARCELLE. No.

ELODIE. I move that we stop doing it.

CHARLES. You want to rewrite the seder?

ELODIE. It's offensive.

CHARLES. Offensive?!?

PATRICK. Personally, I see Elodie's point. Jews? Haggling
over money? Not a good look.

ELODIE. Thank you!

CHARLES. Who asked you? You don't even celebrate Passover.

PATRICK. I'm here, aren't I?

CHARLES. You haven't been to a seder in what, five years?

ELODIE. Which is why he's the perfect person to weigh in –

DANIEL. Can we finish?

CHARLES. But –

DANIEL. Let's finish. Or we'll be here all night.

PATRICK. At this point, despite Elodie's protests, Daniel
and Charles make a show of negotiating for the matzah,
they break it into pieces, we all partake, then Charles
reads:

CHARLES. The injustice of this world still brings to mind
Elijah, who in defense of justice, challenged power.
Elijah opens up the realm of mystery and wonder. Let
us now open the door for Elijah!

> (**DANIEL** *rises to open the door. Before he gets
> too far:)*

MARCELLE. *(Intense.)* NOOOO!!!!!!

Skip this part.

DANIEL. You can't skip this part this is –

MARCELLE. Skip this part, just skip it. We're not doing it this year.

What's next?

DANIEL. But I –

MARCELLE. What comes next?

DANIEL. But I have to open the door –

MARCELLE. Sit! Down!

> *(Beat. **DANIEL** stops moving.)*

CHARLES. Sit down, son.

> *(Beat.)*

ELODIE. But you know he came through her window, he didn't come through the door –

MARCELLE. I don't care.

PATRICK. *(To **MOLLY**.)* She's referencing Halimi. Sarah Halimi. You heard what happened?

MARCELLE. *Doctor* Sarah Halimi, she had a doctorate, she was a doctor.

MOLLY. I don't think so.

PATRICK. She died last week.

MARCELLE. She didn't die. She was killed. *In* her apartment. *In* her apartment. And no one is calling it an act of antisemitism.

CHARLES. A man broke into her apartment. The neighbors heard him scream Allahu Akbar, then he apparently said "I killed the demon."

ELODIE. He went to a different apartment first, he didn't start in her apartment –

MARCELLE. She was the only Jew in her building and she was the only one killed. That's a coincidence? God it's amazing how many coincidences there are in this world.

ELODIE. I didn't say it was a coincidence, I just said he went to a different apartment first, maybe when he realized she was Jewish it added fuel to the fire but he didn't start out looking for someone Jewish. He was insane.

MARCELLE. We are gunned down in our schools, in our supermarkets, now we are thrown out the windows of our own homes.

PATRICK. She was thrown out the window.

MOLLY. Yeah I – I got that.

CHARLES. They don't think she's related to *Ilan* Halimi.

MARCELLE. The fact that they share the same last name *is* a coincidence.

DANIEL. Ilan Halimi's the man who was kidnapped and murdered maybe ten years ago?

MARCELLE. Man? He was twenty-three. Younger than both of you.

DANIEL. They tortured him for three weeks, then dumped his body on the side of the road.

MARCELLE. One percent of the population, we are; and forty percent of the hate crimes. Forty percent! Can you explain that? Can you even fathom it? And Marine Le Pen is going to win enough votes in two weeks to be in the run-off for President of France. Marine Le fucking Pen!

PATRICK. Marine Le Pen is never going to win in the end though, you know that.

MARCELLE. I don't know anything except I begged Daniel not to go out with any visible signs, and now we come to learn you are not safe at home, with the door locked tight. Your own home.

CHARLES. It's OK, dear. It's OK. She's exhausted. She hasn't slept in a week.

PATRICK. Why aren't you sleeping?

MARCELLE. I can't. I can't. I try, I hear a sound. I get up to look, standing in the dark with my flashlight, like a burglar in my own home – there's nothing there, I go back to bed, I hear something else – I can't sleep.

PATRICK. So, take an Ambien.

MARCELLE. Don't make a joke of this.

PATRICK. I'm not.

CHARLES. This isn't a joke.

MARCELLE. I have been… I am the holdout. I am holding everyone back but maybe it's time to listen to… what you all have been trying to tell me. Maybe it's time, if you all, if you all want to leave, maybe it's time for me to listen…

　　　　(Beat.)

PATRICK. Is *that* a joke?

CHARLES. Does she look like she's joking?

PATRICK. Uh… People die every day, Marcelle, let's not lose our minds. A woman got killed. Is it sad? Yes, it's sad. But –

MARCELLE. A Jewish woman was killed, in her home, in Paris, last week. That could have been me.

PATRICK. But it's not! I – I don't even – I – are you serious? Come on, this is bullshit.

CHARLES. It's not bullshit, it happened!

PATRICK. This whole thing is bullshit it's bullshit Marcelle! It's bullshit!

CHARLES. What exactly is bullshit?

PATRICK. I am talking to my sister, not you.

CHARLES. Excuse me?

MARCELLE. Anything you have to say to me you can say to him.

PATRICK. I'll say it in front of him but I don't want to be interrupted by him because I don't –

CHARLES. Oh you don't want to be interrupted –

PATRICK. Because I don't want to hear what he has to say. I don't care what you have to say because you are – he – he – this man – this man has – he brainwashed you.

CHARLES. Excuse me??

MARCELLE. What are you talking about –

PATRICK. He brainwashed you he did he brainwashed you.

CHARLES. Brainwashed! Wow!

PATRICK. We didn't grow up with this bullshit Marcelle I'm sorry but that's what it is it's bullshit. Your seder was nice, your children's bar mitzvahs – very sweet, but it's bullshit. You're smart enough to see that.

CHARLES. What part exactly would you call bullshit –

PATRICK. I am not talking to you I am talking to my sister don't interrupt me.

Before you met him, before you met this man, we – we didn't even grow up Jewish. We're not even – technically we're only half – and technically the wrong half!

MARCELLE. Not only did I consider myself Jewish before I met Charles, I also converted when we married, as you well know, so I am not techincally anything –

PATRICK. We are barely Jews, Marcelle.

MARCELLE. No, *you* are barely a Jew. And with all due respect you raised your daughters to be a quarter of nothing.

PATRICK. That's right! I raised my girls to decide for themselves what to believe. I didn't impose my bullshit on them.

CHARLES. And somehow they turned out militantly secular! How *did* that happen?

MARCELLE. Another coincidence!

PATRICK. Do you hear him, Marcelle, do you hear him?

CHARLES. Do you have a problem with me Patrick?

PATRICK. You have brainwashed my sister and you have put my sister in danger.

CHARLES. Danger!

PATRICK. Yes. We were fine, before she met you, we were *fine.*

CHARLES. Yeah, your family was really thriving in France. Before *I* turned up on the scene, everything was hunky dory.

PATRICK. You're scared in France, so you want to go, where? The Middle East? The most contentious strip of land, in the most volatile region in the world – people are *pouring* out of the Middle East – that's where safety lies?

MARCELLE. So where should we go? Where is safe for us?

PATRICK. And you know where Israelis are going? Berlin!

MARCELLE. Oh perfect!

PATRICK. They're going back to Germany! In droves! They're writing articles about it –

ELODIE. Not in droves, in very small numbers.

PATRICK. They're going back to Germany, so – What does *that* tell you?

MARCELLE. It tells me good for them but they are not my family my concern is for my family so again I ask you, Patrick: Where is safe for us?

PATRICK. Berlin! Here! Wherever!

MARCELLE. No not wherever. That is the point. Where is safe? Tell me! Where can we go to feel safe?

CHARLES. Let's run through the list. Start with A. A. Afghanistan?

MARCELLE. I'll pass.

CHARLES. Argentina? It's not even twenty-five years since they blew up that JCC in Buenos Aires. Eighty-five Jews, blown to smithereens. So, Argentina's out. *Algeria?*

(*Beat.*)

MARCELLE. Where should we go Patrick? Name it for me. Where are Jews safe? Where is my family supposed to go?

DANIEL. I don't want to go anywhere.

(*Quick beat.*)

MARCELLE. Come again?

DANIEL. I don't.

MARCELLE. What are you talking about? You are the reason – you're the *reason* we are doing this –

DANIEL. Don't put this on me.

MARCELLE. Dad took you to Israel, Dad took you to –

DANIEL. No, I *accompanied* Dad to Israel –

MARCELLE. Oh my god such semantics!

CHARLES. I took you to Israel because you don't feel safe here.

DANIEL. No *you* don't feel safe here, I'm not that worried.

PATRICK. Good for you!

CHARLES. Stay out of this Patrick.

MARCELLE. You said you could see yourself living there, you said –

DANIEL. Well I thought about it, and I don't want to leave.

PATRICK. Good for you, Daniel!

CHARLES. Shut UP Patrick.

MARCELLE. You thought about it?

DANIEL. I thought about it.

CHARLES. What happened since you came back, that would make you change your mind? What happened that made you change your mind...

MARCELLE. *(To* **MOLLY**.*)* Get out.

DANIEL. Don't talk to her that way!

MOLLY. We never talk about – not since that first night – not once –

MARCELLE. Get out of my house.

DANIEL. This has nothing to do with Molly!

PATRICK. That's how you treat the stranger in our midst!

MARCELLE. Oh fuck off Patrick –

PATRICK. She's our cousin!

MARCELLE. Our cousin? You didn't know this *cousin* existed until five minutes ago don't call her our cousin like you give a shit.

DANIEL. This has nothing to do with Molly.

MOLLY. We don't discuss it, really.

MARCELLE. I *begged* you to talk to him!

ELODIE. I did talk to him! And her. And I told her to back off –

MOLLY. And I did!

DANIEL. Molly never discussed this with me. I tried – she refused! *She* refused! It's my decision.

ELODIE. Bullshit.

CHARLES. Yes *that's* bullshit, *that's* called bullshit Patrick! *That's* bullshit!

DANIEL. It's not bullshit!

ELODIE. Everyone knows, when you like someone, you're susceptible!

DANIEL. I am not!

ELODIE.	**MARCELLE**.	**CHARLES**.
Uhh... yes!	Yes! You are!	You are.

DANIEL. Oh my god! Everybody! Stop! This is my choice. It's my choice. That's it. OK? That's it. That's...

(**DANIEL** *stands to go, and takes* **MOLLY** *with him. Before she leaves,* **MARCELLE** *stops her.*)

MARCELLE. You care about that boy? He's been beaten in the streets. You saw it yourself. You care about him?

MOLLY. For the record, we never discussed it. Never. Just so you know...

(**MOLLY** *exits after* **DANIEL**. *Everyone watches.*)

CHARLES. You can look down on us, laugh behind our backs – call it bullshit, it makes no difference. Last I checked they don't ask your *personal feelings* when they come knocking. *Hey! This guy thinks it's bullshit, spare him* – no. You get shoved off to the same place we're going.

PATRICK. *(Intense.)* NOT IF THEY DON'T KNOW!!!

> *(Beat.)*

Our father gave us a gift, this is what you did with it? Fuck.

MARCELLE. A gift?

PATRICK. You think he just married Mom? You think that just happened? People just fall in love? People don't just fall in love, Marcelle, that's not how love works. Papa saw things we can never imagine, and then he married – a nice, *Catholic* girl. You think that was an accident? But you knew better, you always know better.

> *(Quick beat.)*

My dear sister, listen to me. There are very few things worth dying for. An old religion is not one of them. You want to draw the curtains once a week and light candles in the dark? No one's going to stop you. But be smart.

My family will still be alive in a hundred years. Will yours?

> *(With that, **PATRICK** leaves. Before he shuts the front door, **MARCELLE** calls out:)*

MARCELLE. Don't close the door. Leave it open. Let Elijah in. And anyone else who wants to come, let them all in.

> *(Lights shift.)*

> *(We join **LUCIEN**, **IRMA**, **ADOLPHE**, and **YOUNG PIERRE**.)*

IRMA. Respectfully, I disagree.

LUCIEN. And I appreciate that, but respectfully – I'm his father.

IRMA. Yes you are.

LUCIEN. I'll decide what's best.

IRMA. Absolutely.

ADOLPHE. Very good.

LUCIEN. Thank you.

> *(Beat.)*

IRMA. It's just –

LUCIEN.	**ADOLPHE**.
Mom...	Irma...

IRMA. A boy his age should be in school. That's all.

LUCIEN. I was his age, when I started working.

IRMA. You were not.

LUCIEN. Close enough.

IRMA. You finished high school. I have your diploma, somewhere.

LUCIEN. Where – In one of your piles?

IRMA. I have your diploma.

LUCIEN. So, clearly that came in handy.

IRMA. He's missed two years, he's so far behind.

LUCIEN. I'll have twice as much work, without Robert.

IRMA. For half as many customers!

LUCIEN. It's still more than I can handle on my own.

IRMA. So you'll hire someone.

LUCIEN. With what money?

IRMA. What good will he be, if he can't do basic math?

LUCIEN. He can do basic math!

IRMA. Or read? Or write?

LUCIEN. He reads. He writes. He's fifteen!

IRMA. No one's buying pianos, Lucien. We're on rations, no one's buying pianos, what's the rush?

ADOLPHE. It'll come back, it came back in '18, after '29…

LUCIEN. He's gonna run the store eventually –

ADOLPHE. It's all circles.

LUCIEN. Might as well learn now, and I need the help so it's as good a time as any for him to start and –

YOUNG PIERRE. What if I don't want to sell pianos?

> *(Beat.)*

LUCIEN. *(Gently.)* Then you won't.

> *(Beat.* **LUCIEN** *is surprised, and defeated.)*

ADOLPHE. Of course, you will do whatever you think is best, and you can do anything, you are more than capable. But it's nice to be at the store, just to be there, because that's the place, you know. It's our place. And it's a nice way to make a living. Work is always hard it always is, but some people work their whole lives, it doesn't mean much to them, and isn't much appreciated by anyone else. Our work brings joy. In homes all across France, children learn to play on pianos from our stores. That's what we do. And it put food on our table.

How lucky are we?

> *(***PATRICK*** *emerges.)*

PATRICK. A few weeks go by. Macron defeats Le Pen. Just like I told everyone he would. I hear nothing from my sister. We aren't speaking. I know – you're shocked. I think about calling…

> *(He looks at his phone.)*

Fuck her. She can call me.

(His phone rings. He considers.)

Fuck her. I don't want talk to her.

(He sends the call to voicemail.)

YOUNG PIERRE. Talk to your sister.

PATRICK. This is an obsession of my father's – talking to my sister.

YOUNG PIERRE. What else is there, once your parents are gone?

PATRICK. All my life, whenever Marcelle and I fought, he'd say:

YOUNG PIERRE. She's your baby sister.

PATRICK. So?

YOUNG PIERRE. You know how rare that is, in this family, to still have your sibling?

IRMA. When my sister died, we were separated by an ocean.

LUCIEN. My brother was killed in another country.

YOUNG PIERRE. My sisters were killed meters from where I stood.

IRMA. I learned she died in a letter. I never said goodbye. I didn't attend her funeral.

LUCIEN. What funeral?

YOUNG PIERRE. I was their kid brother.

IRMA. I have no one left, to talk about my childhood, remember my parents with.

LUCIEN. No one to work beside. Argue with. Rage against.

YOUNG PIERRE. There's no one left to protect me now.

IRMA. I hope it won't always be like this, for our family.

LUCIEN. I hope so, too.

YOUNG PIERRE. I hope so too.

PATRICK. Jesus Christ. What a guilt trip.

YOUNG PIERRE. Just call your sister, sweetheart.

PATRICK. When she wants to talk, she'll call me.

YOUNG PIERRE. She did! You sent it to voicemail!

> *(His phone rings.)*

> *(***YOUNG PIERRE*** *stares at* ***PATRICK***, *desperately hoping he'll answer.)*

PATRICK. *(Gently, to* **YOUNG PIERRE***.)* OK.

> *(***PATRICK*** *answers the phone.)*

(To **MARCELLE***, angrily.)* What!

MARCELLE. We need to talk.

PATRICK. So talk.

She tells me they're leaving –

MARCELLE. We're leaving.

PATRICK. Her, Charles, Elodie.

MARCELLE. Daniel's still deciding.

PATRICK. I tell her: Great! Have a good time!

I say: You don't need my permission.

I say: Is that it?

She says:

MARCELLE. No. There's something else.

PATRICK. I say: What is it? What?

And she says:

MARCELLE. Papa.

> *(Beat. At this moment,* **YOUNG PIERRE***, who has been hovering in the background, moves away.)*

I am of course going to ask him to come with us but –

PATRICK. Never! He's not leaving France! And don't you dare try to drag him away because of –

MARCELLE. I know he won't leave. I know that. I'm going to offer – so he knows he's wanted, he has options… I know he won't take it.

PATRICK. You know what it's called when you make an offer to someone you know they won't accept?

MARCELLE. I –

PATRICK. Bullshit. *That's* called bullshit, Marcelle.

MARCELLE. I'll be back, and – often – it's not far, if he needs me but, you will be the person now, if something comes up –

PATRICK. No.

MARCELLE. Really?

PATRICK. Really.

You want to leave, wash your hands of him? That's on you.

MARCELLE. I'm not washing my hands of him!

PATRICK. I'm not here to alleviate the burden of your guilt. *Don't worry, do whatever you need honey, I've got this.* No, I don't have this. You want to go, go. Bye.

> *(Beat.)*

MARCELLE. You think this is easy? You think this isn't the most impossible thing I have – this is my home. My *home.* This is where – my first words were in French. My whole world everything I think feel say read dream, every friend, every relative I've loved is – I am not some wandering Jew. I have a home. You think this is anything but *agony*?

I have gone out of my way to protect Papa because I know, I saw... since my wedding day I never said a word I never invited him to a single holiday because I saw – I will never forget, waiting in the back of the synagogue to get married, they pass around the basket of kippahs, the basket gets to Papa and he held it in his hand like it was a moon rock, a piece of Mars. And when he put it on his balding head, it didn't lie flat on his skull, it stood up in this weird way, almost on purpose, like he wanted everyone to see it didn't belong on him, it had nothing to do with him. He looked so... frightened, I said, I will never inflict that on him again and I haven't. But now, how do I...

How do I...

How do I tell him, at the end of his life, that his daughter is asking the same question he heard his parents ask when he was a little boy?

How do I tell him?

I... I need to know he will have someone when I... I need to know that. I need to –

PATRICK. He will have someone.

MARCELLE. I need that, Patrick, I need it.

PATRICK. He will have someone.

MARCELLE. And if you would be there when I tell him, so he knows I –

PATRICK. I will be there.

MARCELLE. I just don't want him to feel like I'm, I'm abandoning him, when he needs me most because I could never abandon him I couldn't do that to him, I couldn't, I just, couldn't.

PATRICK. I will be there.

>*(Lights shift.)*

*(**DANIEL** and **MOLLY** appear, out for a walk, maybe stopped on a bridge.)*

*(**DANIEL** takes off his shirt and sings the first verse and chorus of "Forever Young" by Bob Dylan.* If the actor also plays guitar and wants to play, that's fine.)*

*(After he finishes singing, **DANIEL** puts his shirt back on.)*

MOLLY. I should just kill myself right now.

DANIEL. What?!?

MOLLY. *What* is going to top this moment in my life?

DANIEL. Oh.

MOLLY. You don't even know – you can't begin to understand –

DANIEL. Understand what?

MOLLY. It's not – you're French, you won't get it but when I tell people I was *serenaded* by my *boyfriend in Paris*, do you even know? Not that we used that word but for all intents and purposes I had a French boyfriend, in France, in Paris. Do you know how sexy that is where I come from?

DANIEL. You think I'm sexy?

MOLLY. Daniel. For the rest of my life, when someone asks what I did for my twenty-first birthday, I can honestly say I spent it in Paris and my Parisian boyfriend took me to dinner and kissed me on a bridge hanging over the Seine. And I mean, I guess technically we're cousins, but it really is so distant, I won't mention that part.

---

* A license to produce *Prayer for the French Republic* includes permission to perform "Forever Young," subject to a mandatory music fee. Please refer to your licensing agreement for important billing and credit requirements.

DANIEL. How will you say we met?

MOLLY. Who cares? I met you in PARIS! And like, in my wildest dreams, I never pictured that, you know, if I had a French boyfriend he'd be wearing a Yankees hat to hide his yarmulke because he didn't feel safe, but honestly, that is just a minor detail!

DANIEL. Don't leave.

MOLLY. I mean, I should finish college. That seems important.

DANIEL. Eh.

MOLLY. Says the teacher!

DANIEL. Degree, shmegree.

MOLLY. Right, right.

DANIEL. I'll be waiting for you, right here.

MOLLY. Wherever you are.

DANIEL. Here.

MOLLY. Or wherever you are.

DANIEL. You don't mean that.

MOLLY. No?

DANIEL. No, that's not how you feel, I know it.

MOLLY. Oh you do?

DANIEL. I'm staying, OK – no listen – I've decided to –

MOLLY. No, you listen, Daniel, you – you want to know how I feel? Listen, I'll tell you. Every weekend, for a year now, I got on a train and came to Paris, and I'd wonder, *what* was my Great-great-grandma Lucie thinking? How could anyone leave France? My Nana says she wanted adventure, and got a job as a governess for the Rothschild families, maybe that's true. Or, maybe she sensed something, and fled. I'll never know.

But as frightened as I am about the future of my own country, I can't help but feel grateful that she made it her home. Cause if she hadn't? I wouldn't exist.

You go wherever you need to to be safe, because the truth is, you can fight for what's right wherever you are. But you have to be alive to do it.

(Lights shift.)

(ADOLPHE, LUCIEN, *and* **YOUNG PIERRE** *sit together.)*

(Someone is missing.)

(LUCIEN *reaches out to touch his father.* **IRMA** *enters, apart, and speaks to us.)*

IRMA. I am dying in the other room.
　　In fact, I took my last breath just moments ago.
　　It is March 11th, 1946,
　　and for all time,
　　my tombstone will have that date permanently etched onto its stone facade.
　　Even *I* know, there is no sweeter revenge than an old Jew lying in some forgotten graveyard in Europe with a tombstone dated
　　nineteen
　　forty-*six.*
　　Fuck.
　　You.
　　We are hardly religious,
　　but, as is our tradition,
　　I will be buried in a day or two.
　　I could have been buried beside my sister, in America, but we left there long ago.
　　I could have been buried in Havana, or Mexico, had I gone with my daughter, but I didn't.
　　I could have been dumped like so much meat in a pit beside my granddaughters, somewhere in Poland,

but instead,
I'll lie here.
In France.
The country of my birth.
Where my parents are buried,
and their parents,
and their parents before them.
As I fell out of consciousness just now,
I could hear my son Lucien,
consoling Adolphe in the other room,
and that did soothe me,
listening to his voice through the wall.
My life didn't flash before my eyes,
it was more like, things blurred together,
moments profound and mundane:
my fingers on the keyboard of my piano,
the view of France, from the deck of the boat, as we
returned from America,
the key in the mailbox, opening it to discover a
postcard from my sister,
the meals I cooked my family,
the dishes I washed and put away, then took back
down to serve another meal, and washed and put away,
the sound of my husband, up in the middle of the
night, fumbling his way in the dark to the bathroom,
sirens and voices chanting and boots marching in
unison as they pounded the streets of Paris,
paper, turning the page of a book,
dry leaves blowing in a gust of wind and falling to the
ground,
and though I don't pray much
I found myself just now saying a prayer –
it was only a word
but in that one word lives all my hope,
for my family, my country, the future, peace,
acceptance, love and understanding, forward motion,
generations.
As I took my last breath on Earth,

my head resting comfortably on the pillow,
I looked up and said my one-word prayer.
To the ceiling,
and the sky above that,
and to God above it all,
to anyone who might hear
I closed my eyes and I said:
Pierre.

>*(As she says his name, a faint spotlight
>appears on a face we haven't seen:)*
>
>**(PIERRE.***)*
>
>*(He is in his eighties, physically slight, but
>his mind remains sharp as ever.)*
>
>*(As the light grows around him, we see he's
>joined by his family.* **MARCELLE, CHARLES,
>DANIEL, ELODIE,** *and* **PATRICK** *all sit nearby.)*

PIERRE. Why?

MARCELLE. For a lot of reasons. For all the reasons I just
said.

But Patrick isn't going anywhere.

PATRICK. You couldn't *pay* me to move to the Middle East.

MARCELLE. So he'll be here, and it's a very easy flight, and
I'll be back, and of course, anytime you want to visit us,
you can.

>*(***PIERRE** *doesn't say anything.)*

Or not. Up to you.

>*(Still nothing.)*

Papa.

Say something.

PIERRE. What should I say? You do what you need to, honey.

MARCELLE. I know. But I want you to – I want you to know you can come with us.

PIERRE. Why would I come with you?

MARCELLE. If you want. It's an option. If – if you didn't feel safe –

CHARLES. We're concerned it may not be safe here anymore.

PIERRE. It's never been safe. Not anywhere. You know that.

MARCELLE. But it feels like it's starting to get worse.

PIERRE. Yes, it does.

CHARLES. And it could get even worse.

PIERRE. It could. Who knows? No one knows the future. I don't know what will happen fifteen days from now, do you?

CHARLES. We don't, but it doesn't feel like, it doesn't seem like things are headed in a good direction.

PIERRE. Have things ever been headed in a good direction?

France is one of the best countries for Jews, it really is, when you compare it.

PATRICK. It is.

PIERRE. Three-fourths of French Jews survived. You know what a high percentage that is? It was so much worse in Poland, in Germany, Czechoslovakia, Greece. France is the one of the best.

PATRICK. That's absolutely right.

MARCELLE. Patrick.

PATRICK. What?

MARCELLE. Please?

PATRICK. I know – Papa, I know that you've relied on Marcelle for a lot of things over the years, and so –

PIERRE. I have not!

MARCELLE. Not relied on – but I've helped, I've, I've been there –

PIERRE. No one's helped me, I've done just fine on my own.

CHARLES. What he's trying to say –

MARCELLE. Forget it, forget it –

PATRICK. What we're trying to say is, I'm not going anywhere, I'm staying right here in Paris, so, anything you need, you come to me.

(**PIERRE** *makes a sarcastic sound.*)

Nice.

(*Beat.*)

CHARLES. We are just trying to do what's best for the children.

PIERRE. Well you have to. You have to. Is this about me? Don't worry about me. My mother, she refused to leave without Grandfather Nathan, but he was too old to travel, so we stayed, and that was not a good decision. Old people are such a pain in the ass that way, you know?

MARCELLE. So, Papa: We are leaving before the end of summer.

CHARLES. Doctors can transfer their degrees now, Marcelle and I should both be able to practice.

PIERRE. And you will teach?

MARCELLE. I will have to give that up.

CHARLES. For now.

MARCELLE. For forever, probably.

CHARLES. You don't know.

MARCELLE. I know.

I still have to learn Hebrew fluently, which…

PIERRE. You can learn. Our cousins came back from the war speaking beautiful Spanish. And they hadn't spoken a word when they left.

(*To* **ELODIE.**) This one will learn in two seconds, she's so bright. A change will be good for you, I think.

ELODIE. I think so too.

DANIEL. And the store?

CHARLES. What about it?

DANIEL. That's it? That's the end? We're just gonna let it die?

ELODIE. He's right here, Daniel, he's still running it.

DANIEL. Almost two centuries, five generations – no one cares?

MARCELLE. Of course we care, of course I do –

DANIEL. No one wants to keep it going?

PATRICK. You want to run a piano store?

DANIEL. Maybe.

MARCELLE. Patrick – no – Daniel –

DANIEL. Maybe I do!

MARCELLE. You do not! You don't even like pianos, you play guitar –

DANIEL. Well maybe I want to sell them –

MARCELLE. You don't know what you want!

CHARLES. Marcelle.

MARCELLE. He doesn't! You want to be Orthodox, you want to be a math teacher, you want to live in Israel, you want to sell pianos –

DANIEL. I never said I want to live to Israel I never said that!

CHARLES. OK well I don't have the *transcript* handy but it certainly seemed to me like you wanted to go –

MARCELLE. That's why we're going! That's the whole reason! For you! We're going for –

DANIEL. For yourselves. For yourselves.

(**PIERRE** *holds up his hand and laughs. Somehow, this quiets everyone.*)

PIERRE. I feel like I'm fifteen again.

PATRICK. They're loud, huh?

MARCELLE. Shut up Patrick.

PATRICK. Why don't you shut up?

PIERRE. You want to sell pianos?

MARCELLE. Of course he doesn't.

PIERRE. It's a difficult life.

DANIEL. I know.

MARCELLE. No! This is not – we are not doing this –

PATRICK. Papa's trying to speak will you let Papa speak.

(**PIERRE** *turns to* **DANIEL.**)

PIERRE. You don't want to run the store. *I* didn't want to.

(*The* **FAMILY** *looks at* **PIERRE.** *They were not expecting him to say this.*)

The store is why we didn't leave. We couldn't. We would have starved. Everything we had was in those pianos. So we stayed. And paid the price.

Of course, I survived, and why? Papa. Right from the start, I was 154982, he was 154983, and that's how it was the whole time, always he was right behind me. I wouldn't have made it otherwise, because Papa was an optimist. He was a natural born salesman. Not like me. I'm a pessimist. But Papa always stayed hopeful.

That first winter, he said, "don't worry, we'll be home for Christmas." But December came and went, we were still in Poland, that year *and* the next. Then spring came, 1945, we were liberated, by Christmas we *were* back in Paris – and my father turned to me with a big grin and said, "See. I told you we'd be home."

Then Papa wanted me to come work with him. He didn't understand my resistence. I couldn't tell him, each night before bed, I heard my mother's voice, calling out from wherever people go when they're gone: "Forget the pianos. Learn something you can do anywhere. Study, Pierre. Study engineering. That's right."

I didn't know what to do. But in the end, I went with Papa. There's no good reason. I just wanted to be near him. Because once Grandfather Adolphe died, I was all he had and he was all I had. And we were together like that until the day I married your grandmother. I went from one optimist's home to another, and that was good for me. I needed that.

Because after '45, no one wanted to hear about the war. But at the store, I could keep them all alive. I could hang a picture of Colette, presenting flowers to the President of France, Albert Lebrun. And you know something? No one has ever looked at the photo and asked, "where's your sister?"

Papa has been dead more than fifty years. I have kept the store going all this time, longer than anyone who came before me. And once again, Papa has saved my life, because if I had become an engineer, at some office, I would have felt very alone. Instead, I go to work each day, I see the pianos, the old advertisements, I see our name on the door, and I know they are with me. And I go on.

Stay together. Stay with your parents. You have to. In the end, it saved my life.

(*Beat.*)

MARCELLE. Papa.

PIERRE. It's alright, sweetheart.

MARCELLE. I just... I wish I knew, knew for sure what the right thing to do was, I... Do you think we – am I a coward?

PIERRE. No. No.

You have to trust your instincts, that's all you have. If your instincts tell you time to go, it's time to go.

You must go with your parents, yes?

DANIEL. Yes.

(**PIERRE** *touches* **DANIEL.** *He takes a long moment to think. Then he looks up at him.*)

PIERRE. Daniel. You're a thinking person: why do they hate us?

DANIEL. I don't know, Grandpa.

(*There's a long beat, as they all sit there, letting the question linger.*)

Cause we're different?
We're not like them?

And we don't want to be like them...
And they don't understand why...

ELODIE. Is it because they think we think we're better than
them?
In which case, they'll show us.
Or do they think we know something they don't?
In which case, what *exactly* do we know?
They hate us for that.

CHARLES. It's because of Christ?
They hate us for killing him.

ELODIE. We didn't kill Christ.

CHARLES. I know, but –

ELODIE. They made us slaves in Egypt long before Christ.

CHARLES. I know, but then they hated us for "killing" him.
Then they hated us for not believing in him.
Then they just hated us so they made us do the most
unholy thing they could think of: lend money,
and when we learned to do that, they hated us for
learning how to do something they forced us to do.

PATRICK. It's about money.
When we have it, they hate us for having it.
When we don't, they hate us for being poor, filthy,
disgusting, a drain on society.
They hate us for being capitalists,
they hate us for being communists.
It doesn't matter.
If it has to do with money,
they need someone to blame, so they blame us.
Then they hate us.

CHARLES. They hate us when we live in their countries,
they hate us when we make our own country.

ELODIE. They hate us for controlling everything,
which is confusing, cause they've been pretty
successful at killing us the last two thousand years,
if we controlled everything wouldn't we have done a
better job of at least controlling how often they kill us?

But.
Most of all,
they hate us because they cannot understand how we
are still here.
How is it possible?
We have been attacked,
beaten,
burned,
converted,
expelled,
robbed,
raped,
gassed,
enslaved,
tortured,
for thousands of years,
and still, we are here.
We are still here.
How?
Are we all Houdinis?
Saw us in half, somehow we're still alive.
Annihilate us in your gas chambers,
we'll send back Elie Wiesel, Primo Levi,
even our dead girls' diaries are masterpieces.
The world wants us dead and in return what do we
give them?
Einstein and Freud,
Kafka and Proust,
Arendt, Chagall.
Names that ring out like planets,
Universes of thought and genius.
And still,
they hate
hate
hate
hate us.

    (Beat.)

DANIEL. But I won't hate them back.

(**MARCELLE** *goes to* **DANIEL**.)

MARCELLE. And we won't.
OK?
We won't.
It's gonna be great. OK?
Hey – it's gonna be great.

(*Lights shift.* **PATRICK** *speaks to us as the stage clears.*)

PATRICK. I was not there, later that summer, the morning they left, to say goodbye. They packed their things, took almost all the furniture, save the piano. Too heavy to transport. And there's no room for it at my place. We'll have to bring it to my father's store, on Rue du Fabourg Montmartre, so he can try to sell it. Pianos Salomon spans five generations, it has been open more than a hundred and sixty years, and you can find my father there Tuesdays through Saturdays, eleven to noon, two-thirty to seven.

(**MARCELLE'S FAMILY** *scatters, taking things offstage. It's mostly cleared, save the piano.* **MARCELLE** *makes a final inventory, when* **CHARLES**, **DANIEL**, *and* **ELODIE** *enter, wheeling suitcases.*)

(**CHARLES** *approaches the piano, takes out a croissant, rips it into four pieces, and divides it among his family.*)

CHARLES. This is the bread of affliction,
the poor bread,
which our ancestors ate,
in the land of – France.

(*They eat.*)

DANIEL. These aren't even that good.

(They all start to leave, except **MARCELLE.***)*

MARCELLE. Be right there.

*(***MARCELLE*** *takes one final moment alone, as* **PATRICK** *stands on the other side of the stage.)*

PATRICK. I love you with all my heart Marcelle, though you won't hear me say it. You'll be ten thousand meters in the air when I think of it, I know what time your flight is and I'll look up, hoping to see your plane, before it crosses the Mediterranean, in the latest incarnation of our family's wanderings.

I don't know what will become of her, of me, of France, of the world. But I am rooting for her, and all the wanderers of the Earth. There will be many more in the years to come, from all walks of life, and I am rooting for them – for all of us. And I will say a prayer – yes, even me, your nonbelieving brother. What is a prayer anyway, but speaking aloud your hope?

*(***MARCELLE*** *is about to go, when* **LUCIEN** *[or* **IRMA** *or* **ADOLPHE,** *depending on the actor who plays best] comes to the piano and plays a gentle version of "La Marseillaise."* **PIERRE** *joins and sings:)*

PIERRE.
ALLONS ENFANTS DE LA PATRIE
LE JOUR DE GLOIRE EST ARRIVÉ!

*(***PATRICK*** *joins in, as the* **ANCESTORS** *gather around the piano.* **MARCELLE** *watches.)*

PIERRE & LUCIEN.
CONTRE NOUS DE LA TYRANNIE,
L'ÉTENDARD SANGLANT EST LEVÉ

**PATRICK, IRMA, ADOLPHE, LUCIEN, PIERRE
& YOUNG PIERRE.**
L'ÉTENDARD SANGLANT EST LEVÉ
ENTENDEZ-VOUS DANS LES CAMPAGNES
MUGIR CES FÉROCES SOLDATS?
ILS VIENNENT JUSQUE DANS VOS BRAS
ÉGORGER VOS FILS, VOS COMPAGNES!

(**MARCELLE** *exits, as they sing:*)

AUX ARMES, CITOYENS!
FORMEZ VOS BATAILLONS!
MARCHONS, MARCHONS!
QU'UN SANG IMPUR
ABREUVE NOS SILLONS!

(*The* **ANCESTORS** *stand in silent guard.*)

(*Then:*)

(*Blackout.*)

End of Play

www.ingramcontent.com/pod-product-compliance
Lightning Source LLC
Chambersburg PA
CBHW071927130726
47909CB00014B/2615